Christmas Chaos

A Shandra Higheagle Mystery Novella

Paty Jager

Windtree Press

Corvallis, OR

This is a work of fiction, Names, characters, places, and incidents either are the product of the author's imagination or are used fictitiously, and any resemblance to actual persons living or dead, business establishments, events, or locales, is entirely coincidental.

Shandra Higheagle Mystery Books

Double Duplicity
Tarnished Remains
Deadly Aim
Murderous Secrets
Killer Descent
Reservation Revenge
Yuletide Slaying
Fatal Fall
Haunting Corpse
Artful Murder
Dangerous Dance
Homicide Hideaway
Toxic Trigger-point
Abstract Casualty
Capricious Demise
Vanishing Dream

This novella is for the fans who kept asking for more Shandra Higheagle books. I hope this will finally bring you closure on the series.

If you are picking this up and haven't read the Shandra Higheagle Mystery series yet, hopefully, this will make you want to go back and start with book one, *Double Duplicity* where Shandra and Ryan meet.

Chapter One

Shandra Higheagle Greer smiled as she glanced around at her handiwork. The twins, Jayden and Mia, would be arriving in Huckleberry tomorrow. She had the house all decorated except for the tree, which they would cut, bring down the mountain, and decorate the day after the two arrived.

This would be their tenth Christmas together. What a blessing the twins had been coming into her and Ryan's life when they did. She felt bad for the reason, their father, and who they thought of as a mother, had been killed. First, Shandra and Ryan had fostered the two and then adopted them.

Jayden had been the harder of the two to open up and see that his new parents were different from the ones he'd known and that they expected him to only be a child and grow confident. He had played football and been better, many said, than his biological father. While he could have received an academic scholarship at Washington State University in Pullman, Washington, he'd opted for a football scholarship. When they talked with him, he sounded as if he was thriving in the environment. He was studying to be in law enforcement.

Mia was also attending WSU only on an academic scholarship. She was in the nursing program. Shandra was proud of how hard the two worked for their scholarships, not wanting to burden her and Ryan for money to continue their education.

Shandra knew they felt they had a lot to prove. In a small community like Weippe County, many people remembered their parents, and not always in a good way.

A scratch at the back of the house

started Shandra heading to the back door. She caught herself, remembering Sheba had passed over six months ago. Every time there was a thump or a scratch, she found herself going to let the dog in. Being alone out here was hard to get used to. She'd always had Lil and Sheba for company.

Lil had finally married Claude at the feed store and no longer lived on the ranch. With her helper and Sheba gone, Shandra had to go to the corral and visit the horses for company these days. Though Mia's cat Saphire was more than willing to lay on her lap in a chair on the patio when the cat was around.

Dream a Little Dream, tinkled from her phone. Shandra smiled.

"Hello, Ryan. Does this mean you can get away and help me decorate?" she answered.

His chuckle warmed her heart. "I could send my sisters over to help if you like."

"I don't need the help. I would like my husband's company."

"Are you sure you'll be okay spending the night by yourself?" Ryan asked, concern deepening his voice and wrapping her in the love he showed her every day.

"I've spent nights here by myself before. Ever since we all moved to your house in Warner when the twins started high school, I've spent time here by myself working on my pottery."

"No, you had Lil dropping by and helping. And now you don't even have Sheba to talk to."

She heard the sadness in his voice. For all his talk about Sheba's cowardice, Ryan had loved the dog as much as she had.

Shandra sighed and said, "I miss Sheba, Jayden, Mia, and you. I can't wait for you and the twins to get here tomorrow."

"I bet you have the house all decorated."

"I do. All that is left is getting the tree. I remember the first Christmas we had the twins. It was like they'd never had a Christmas before." She thought of how the two had been in awe of her decorations and the ritual of going up the mountain to cut a tree. Then bringing it home to decorate, while eating donuts and drinking hot chocolate. It had become a tradition.

"Don't forget to pick up the donuts tomorrow on your way through Huckleberry," Shandra said.

"That's at the top of my list."

"You have a list?" Shandra teased. As the sheriff of Weippe County, Idaho, he had a lot more responsibility than when she'd met him. Then he was a new hire detective for the Sheriff's Department. Lucky for her, he saw she was innocent when the Huckleberry Police Officer put her in handcuffs without seeking all the facts.

"I have two lists. One for the county and one for my family."

"Does the list for family also say to be home on time?" When he was on a case as a detective he would work long hours, but as the sheriff, he felt he had to be doing that job and helping the new detective learn the ropes as well as keep the deputies happy. Even when she was in Warner, she saw very little of him. "You promised you would spend every day the twins are home with us."

"Unless there is a murder or pile up on the highway, you will all three have my undivided attention." He said something muffled, and then added, "I have to go. I'll see you tomorrow."

"I'm looking forward to it." Shandra ended the call and walked into the kitchen. She heated up a bowl of soup and sat down to eat it as she fiddled with a drawing she'd been thinking of painting on a vase.

~*~

Ella, Grandmother, hovered above a red spot in the middle of a pristine white world. Shandra looked around. She stood on the side of a road and realized the red spot was melting the snow. A noise caught her attention. She stared in that direction and recognized the license plate and school mascot sticker in the back window of the vehicle. Why was Jayden and Mia's car sitting here? She glanced at the red spot. Fear squeezed her chest. "Why Ella?" she whispered.

Shandra sat up in bed shaking and wishing she had Ryan or Sheba to cling to. But all that met her was a silent, cold, dark bedroom. She pulled on a fleece robe and slid her feet into slippers. Walking out to the kitchen she glanced at the clock on the wall. 2:17.

Making a cup of tea and digging a notepad and pen out of a drawer, Shandra returned to the great room and started the propane fireplace. She pulled a chair up close and started writing down everything she could remember about the dream. When she had all the information down, she sat back sipping her tea, and wondered why, after eleven years, Ella showed up in her dream tonight.

Chapter Two

Ryan reached for his cell phone on the bedside table before he was completely awake. "Greer," he answered, trying to make the blurry red numbers on the bedside clock come into focus. It appeared to be 3 a.m.

"Ryan, sorry to bother you but there's been an incident outside of Huckleberry and your kids are involved," Deputy Ron Trapp said.

"Jayden and Mia?" Ryan sat up and shoved the covers off. "Are they hurt?"

"They aren't, but the young woman who was riding with them. She's dead. Ryan, it doesn't look good."

His deputy's words didn't make sense. If the kids were okay, why didn't it look good? And if they were okay, why was a young woman dead?

"Where did this happen?" he asked, wondering what the kids were doing headed home tonight. They hadn't expected them until tomorrow.

"The body was found on County Road 15," Ron said, then his voice muffled as he spoke to someone.

"Is that where the kids are?" It made sense they were headed home. Shandra would want to comfort the twins.

"Their vehicle was towed and I have them in my car. I'll take them to Huckleberry. Their story is kind of fuzzy. Doesn't make sense. I think you need to talk to them. At a police station."

Ryan didn't like the sound of that. "I'll be at the Huckleberry Station in thirty." He hung up, and as he dressed debated whether or not to call Shandra. If he didn't, she'd be mad.

As he settled into his SUV and started the vehicle, he called Shandra.

She answered immediately. "It's the twins."

"How did you know?" he asked.

"Grandmother came to me in a dream. She showed me their car and blood on the snow. Are they hurt?"

"Ron says they aren't hurt but a girl who was with them is dead and I need to question the twins. He said it didn't look good." That phrasing bothered Ryan.

"Where are they being taken?" Shandra asked.

"Huckleberry Police."

"I'll meet you there."

The line went dead. Ryan didn't have a doubt in his mind that she would be at the station requesting to see the kids when he arrived.

~*~

Shandra parked her aging Jeep around the corner from the police station. She took a deep breath telling herself she would be strong and confident. The twins would need her strength. Stepping out of her car, she spotted Ryan's vehicle pull up to the front of the building.

She hurried over.

He gave her a one-armed hug as they walked into the building together.

"Where are they?" Ryan asked the young woman sitting at the dispatch desk.

"Deputy Trapp has them in the conference room," she said, her gaze on Shandra.

Ryan grasped Shandra's hand and led her down the hall. She had a hard time not running ahead of him. It had only been a few months since she'd seen the twins, but knowing they had possibly witnessed a person's death could have triggered visions of what Jayden had witnessed of his father's and aunt's deaths.

"We'll go in together, but you will have to stay quiet until I get the information from Ron." Ryan stopped at the door and studied her.

Shandra gulped down the frustration and nodded. When the lump in her throat finally slid down enough she could talk, she said, "I'll wait, but can I hug them?"

A smile tipped his lips. "Yes, you can give them a hug. Just don't ask any questions."

She nodded and he opened the door.

Her heart ached to see the fear and anxiety on Jayden and Mia's faces. Shandra crossed the room and leaned down between the two sitting in chairs. She pulled them each into an arm and hugged them. "Everything will be okay," she said.

She glanced at Ryan who was talking in a low voice with Deputy Trapp.

"I couldn't believe it—" Mia started.

Shandra shook her head. "You can't tell me anything until you talk to Ryan and Deputy Trapp."

Mia's eyes widened. "Are we in trouble?"

"No, you aren't in trouble," Ryan said, taking a seat across the table from them.

Shandra peered into Ryan's eyes. She could tell whatever Ron had told him wasn't good for the kids.

Ron drew a chair over for Shandra to sit on between the twins. She gave him a smile of thanks and sat, holding hands with Mia and Jayden.

Ryan's gaze settled on Jayden. "Jayden, can you tell me where you met," he consulted a log book in front of him, "Holly Garvie?"

Jayden glanced at his sister. "Ask Mia."

Mia clenched Shandra's hand. "She is- was a girl from school. She was in a dorm room on my floor. She heard where I lived and asked if we could give her a ride to Huckleberry. Then her family would pick her up and take her to Missoula."

"How did she end up on the county road if you left her in Huckleberry?" Ryan asked.

Shandra raised an eyebrow. She hadn't seen the twins' car on her drive to Huckleberry.

Mia squeezed Shandra's hand. "We

don't know. It doesn't make sense. We were sitting in Rigatoni's waiting for Holly's parents to pick her up. After an hour she received a text message, said goodbye her ride was outside, and left. We finished our desserts, I used the restroom, and started for home."

"Mia had dozed off and I saw something on the side of the road," Jayden took up the story. "I couldn't tell what it was but I saw blood. I was going to go on by thinking someone had hit a deer when I saw a hand raise. I slammed on the brakes—"

"Which woke me up," Mia added. "I said that looks like Holly's coat."

"We both got out and it was Holly," Jayden said, peering at his sister.

Mia's hand clenching Shandra's was white. Her face had paled. "Her face was smashed and her-her…" Mia gulped.

"She looked like someone had taken a sledgehammer to her head," Jayden said, his voice devoid of emotion.

Shandra could see he was shutting

down. Memories of finding his father full of buckshot and the woman he knew as his mother dead with slit wrists had to be flashing in his mind.

"It's okay. Ryan and Deputy Trapp just need the facts so they can find out what happened to Holly," Shandra said, trying to convey to her husband that the twins needed to be handled differently than most witnesses.

Ryan didn't smile, but his eyes held sympathy and a look she'd seen before. There was something he was holding back. Was it something about the young woman or something the kids weren't saying?

"Jayden, why did you tell Deputy Trapp and us right now that it looked like she'd been hit by a sledgehammer?" Ryan asked.

Shandra's mind spun. Had that been what was used on Holly? It took clenching her jaw tight to keep from asking.

"Because of," he swallowed as if trying to keep something down in his throat.

"The shape of the bruises, torn skin, and

the amount of broken facial bones," Mia finished.

Jayden glared at her. "You say it as if you're an expert. You aren't. You've only had a trimester of college and that's for nursing, not forensics."

Mia leaned around Shandra. "But I've been reading all the books I could find on forensics and what weapons can do to bodies."

Shandra gently settled Mia in her chair. "I thought you were in the nursing program?"

Mia's cheeks reddened. "I've decided I want to be a forensic pathologist. Professor Spark said he thinks I'd make a very good one."

Shandra had to admit, Mia had the mind for solving puzzles. "I'm glad you found someone at the college who is helping you."

Ron cleared his throat. "If Holly's family picked her up in Huckleberry, what was she doing on the county road and not the highway to Missoula?"

Jayden shrugged.

Mia made invisible circles on the table with her forefinger. "We didn't really see what vehicle—"

"If one did pick her up," Jayden cut in.

Ryan jumped into the conversation. "What makes you say that?" His gaze was on Jayden.

"The table we sat in at the restaurant was near the window. I didn't see any car lights pull up to the curb before Holly said she got a text that her dad was there. Then after she left, I never saw any lights move out into the street."

Ryan leaned his forearms on the table and studied the twins. Ron said he'd found a wood-splitting axe flung into the snow bank not twenty feet from the body. He thought it interesting that the first words out of Jayden's mouth were, "It looks like she was hit with a sledgehammer."

"The two of you didn't see Holly actually get into a vehicle?" Ryan asked, scanning their faces.

"No," Jayden said.

Mia shook her head.

Ryan turned to Ron. "Did you find her cell phone on her?"

"Nothing. Not even identification. Just a purse, which Mia said was the one the victim had with her when they left the college."

"What about a backpack or suitcase?" Shandra asked before Ryan had a chance to ask. He flashed a look at his wife but knew it would do no good to tell her to keep quiet. These were the two children she'd fought hard to find and keep after they'd been in one of her dreams involving her deceased grandmother.

"She only had her purse. When I asked why she didn't bring any clothes, Holly said she had plenty at home and didn't see any reason to haul them back and forth." Mia shrugged as if it made sense to her.

Ryan caught his wife's gaze. What young woman would not pack at least a cosmetic bag? Mia used little makeup but she always took a toiletry bag of shampoo, conditioner, body wash, toothbrush and paste, various facial cleansers, and lotions. He knew for a fact she packed all of that stuff when she went to college over three months before.

Ryan worried the twins had been used to get Holly away from the college to elope or runaway, not to go home. And it turned out bad.

"Did Holly have a boyfriend she talked about?" Ryan asked.

Shandra gave him a slight nod. It appeared his wife was thinking the same thing.

Mia glanced at Jayden.

Ryan didn't miss the exchange between the twins. As they grew older, he'd noticed this exchange less and less but here it was. A possibility that Jayden and the dead girl had been dating. Another piece of evidence the D.A. could use to make a case against his son.

Jayden glared at his sibling and said,

"Mia gave Holly the stupid idea that if she pretended she was dating me, the guy who was bugging her would leave her alone."

Shandra's intake of breath drew Ryan's gaze to her. She peered into his eyes. His smart wife had just realized there was a lot of evidence against their two children. And if someone dug up the past, the siblings could end up in court for the murder of Holly Garvie.

Ryan had no doubt Shandra's grandmother would help them find the real killer before Jayden and Mia's lives were tainted by a false arrest for murder.

Chapter Three

Shandra felt Mia's nails digging into her hand. Her daughter still clung to her right hand, but Jayden had released her left. When he'd told Ryan about the situation his sister put him in, he'd dropped Shandra's hand as if she'd also been in on the subterfuge.

"Did this boy leave Holly alone after she'd pretended she was dating your brother?" Ryan asked Mia.

Tears glistened in Mia's eyes. She hiccupped and said, "He picked a fight with Jayden."

Shandra put a hand on her son's shoulder. "He beat you up?" She studied his face, looking for traces of bruising or cuts.

"He came out the loser. He's not too bright. He waited for me outside the locker room and lit into me after practice. Half the team pulled him off me and then gave him a whipping." A smile barely tipped the corners of his mouth as he remembered the fight.

"Did you get in trouble?" Shandra asked.

"No. The whole team vouched for me that he started it and I didn't touch him." He shook his head. "When everyone on the team said they hit him, the coach couldn't do anything if they wanted enough players for the next game." He shifted his gaze from Shandra to Ryan. "I told the team they didn't have to say they all did it, but they said we were a team and no one beat up on a member of the team and got away with it."

Shandra could tell it had meant a lot to Jayden to have the whole team stick up for him. The local kids, being fed lies from their parents, hadn't treated Jayden or Mia very nice when they went back to school after the murders of their parents were cleared up. Jayden had excelled as an athlete and an academic which caused jealousy. Parents and his teammates would talk trash about his father, whose footsteps he was following.

"What is this kid's name?" Ryan asked.

"Skylar Botts," Mia said, shuddering.

Mia's hand trembled in Shandra's. "What don't you like about him?" she asked in a soft voice.

"He looks at girls with an odd stare. It makes my skin crawl." Mia rubbed her hands up and down her arms as if she were cold. "And he can't say anything without making it sound crude."

Shandra shot a glance at Ryan. She could tell by his furrowed brow and intense gaze on Mia he was interested in the way the young man made his daughter feel. Mia had proven in several instances to have good instincts about people.

"What happened to Skylar after the fight?" Ryan asked.

Jayden shrugged. "I don't know. I didn't

have any classes with him and never saw him after he started the fight."

Shandra could see Jayden was telling them the truth. She'd learned when they first found the two hiding in the woods that he told the truth unless he thought someone else, a family member or someone he cared about, would get in trouble.

Ryan shifted his gaze to Mia. "Did he bother Holly anymore?"

She nodded. "He showed up at the dorm bandaged and bruised and told Holly, 'Both of them would pay.'"

"Did she tell anyone about this threat?" Ryan asked.

Shandra worried that if he had killed Holly, the girl he liked, he might also want to kill Jayden. She reached out, grasping his hand. He must have felt her tremors because he focused on her.

"What's wrong, Mom?" His dark brown eyes softened as he gazed at her.

"Nothing. I think all of this just hit me." She gave him a smile, and he squeezed her hand.

"You two go home with Shandra and stay there. We'll need to test your car," Ryan said.

"Our car didn't cause her death," Jayden said, his eyes narrowing on Ryan.

"We need to check everything we can to prove you didn't do it," Ryan stood and walked over to Shandra and the twins. "I know you didn't harm Miss Garvie. But many would say I'm biased because I'm your father. We have to treat this death just like we do all of them. Your car will be impounded and checked for the victim's blood and hair on the outside. You told us she rode in the car, so there isn't any reason to worry about us finding her hair or anything she left behind." He put a hand on Jayden's arm. "I'll do some digging and see what I can discover about Skylar Botts and Holly's family."

Shandra mouthed thank you to Ryan and also stood. The twins followed her from the room and out to her Jeep. "Let's get home and I'll make us all a cup of hot chocolate before we try to get some sleep."

After the twins grabbed their bags out of Jayden's car, Mia slid into the backseat of the Jeep. She sniffled and said, "It doesn't seem right to slide in the back seat and not have to move Sheba over."

Shandra met her daughter's gaze in the rearview mirror. "I wish she was drooling over my shoulder every time I get in."

~*~

By the time they drove up the driveway, the muted winter sun spread a faint glow over the snowy meadow Shandra called home.

"Do you two want to just go to bed?" Shandra asked as they entered the mudroom they'd built onto the house when they also added another bedroom after adopting the twins.

"Not yet. I'm hungry," Jayden said, dropping his backpack in his room.

"I could eat something," Mia said, disappearing into her room to drop her bag on her bed.

"Then I guess I should pop the cinnamon rolls I have rising in the fridge into the oven." She smiled as Mia and Jayden high-fived.

She pulled the pan of rolls that she'd made the night before out of the fridge and placed them on the counter next to the stove. Turning the dial to preheat the oven, she smiled. Even though the twins had been gone only a few months, it felt good to be taking care of them again.

"Would you both like hot chocolate while you wait?" She moved to the cupboard that held the Christmas-themed mugs.

"Sounds good," Jayden said, sliding onto his usual stool at the island.

"Do you have whipped cream?" Mia asked, heading for the refrigerator.

"Of course!" Shandra grinned. "And marshmallows." She still remembered the first time they'd brought the two to the house. Lil had warmed to them right away and had piled tiny marshmallows in the kids' hot chocolate.

"Do Ryan and Deputy Trapp think we killed Holly?" Jayden asked.

The sorrow in his voice tugged at Shandra's heart. "No, they just need to know all the facts so they can find out who did." She put an arm around her son's shoulders. "You know Ryan will do everything to find the person who took Holly's life."

"Is it bad to hope it is Skylar?" Mia asked.

"Because you're scared of him?" Shandra asked, hoping her daughter would tell her more about the reactions she felt around the young man.

"That and he tried to hurt Jayden. All the girls think he's creepy. Clare said he tried to grab her one night on her way from a late lab." Mia's nose wrinkled. "But Clare can't always be believed. She makes stuff up to get attention."

"What about Holly? Was she secretive?" Shandra pulled the pan of hot chocolate off the stove as the preheat buzzer sounded. She stirred the drink as she poured it into the mugs.

"I guess. Kind of. But I believe her when she said Skylar was getting more and more forceful about her going out with him." Mia pulled a filled cup over to her and made a whipped cream mountain on her drink.

Jayden dropped marshmallows into his mug, watching each one drop.

Shandra moved to the oven, inserted the cinnamon rolls, and set the timer. Taking her mug of hot chocolate, she pulled a chair to the end of the island where she could watch both of the twins. "Have either of you made friends at school?" She wanted to take their minds off what had happened and perhaps get a little more out of them about Holly.

Chapter Four

Ryan arrived at the house around noon. He'd planned to head home as soon as he'd finished talking to the Garvies and putting Ron to work getting all the information he could about Skylar Botts. However, he'd learned some interesting things from the Garvies. Information that he'd followed up on and then handed over to his sister, Cathleen, who worked county dispatch and did research.

He walked into the quiet house and discovered Shandra wrapped in a blanket on the couch.

"Ryan, I didn't think we'd see you until

tonight," Shandra said, sitting up. He could tell she'd been trying to catch up on sleep. Or trying to get more information from her grandmother.

"Are the kids sleeping?" he asked in a quiet voice as he sat when Shandra scooted over and patted the leather cushion.

"Yes. We had cinnamon rolls and hot chocolate when we returned. They were tired but worried too. I think being normal helped them to settle down and not—"

"No! No! Don't!" Jayden's shouts rang down the hall.

"Not again," Ryan said, jolting from the couch and jogging to Jayden's bedroom. The boy had battled nightmares for three years after he'd found his father and aunt's murdered bodies. As much as he said he wanted to do police work if seeing a body like Holly's was going to bring on nightmares, Jayden needed to be persuaded to go into another profession.

Ryan opened the door and found Jayden sitting up against the headboard. The young man hugged his pillow. Sitting on the edge of the bed, Ryan restrained from touching his son. Jayden wasn't a touchy-feely young man despite the tears trickling down the sides of his face.

"It's okay. We're going to find out who killed Holly," Ryan said in a quiet tone.

Jayden shook his head. "I'm not—it isn't—when will seeing something like that not bring back the images of my dad?" The anguish in his voice tore at Ryan.

"We may need to find you a therapist in Pullman." Ryan put a hand on his son's arm. "And you may need to think about another profession."

Jayden wiped a hand across his eyes and nodded. "My roommate said I had a nightmare the night after we were shown some graphic photos in one of my classes." He peered into Ryan's eyes. "I wanted to be a detective like you and help catch the bad people."

"I think you need to find something where you aren't going to be reminded of what you saw as a child." Ryan patted his knee. "I'm sure your mom can come up with all kinds of things for you to change your focus to."

Jayden smiled and snickered. "She told me I'd make a good chef, but I'd have to give up my football scholarship and go to a different college."

"I'm sure the two of you could come up with something that is available at WSU." Ryan stood. "If you've had enough sleep you could come out and help me get the sled ready for tree cutting tomorrow."

Jayden drew in a breath, let it out slowly, and tossed the pillow to the side. "You know walking into the woods and getting the tree is my favorite part of this holiday." He waved to the door. "I'll be out in a few minutes."

Ryan smiled, glad that as an almost adult, Jayden could cast away the fear and gloom his nightmares brought on. "Dress warm. I think the sled will need to be ridden down the hill to see if it can hold a tree."

"Yeah?" Jayden's face lit up.

Chuckling, Ryan entered the great room and found Mia sitting on the couch next to Shandra.

"Is Jayden okay?" Mia asked.

"He'll be fine." He smiled at Mia and shifted his attention to Shandra. "He may need your help in finding a different degree to pursue."

Shandra nodded. "I wondered about that from the start. We'll talk about it while he's home on break."

"Let's get that sled ready to go," Jayden said, entering the room dressed in the snowsuit he wore when skiing.

"I haven't had time to change. I'll be back in five minutes." Ryan entered the bedroom he and Shandra shared.

Shandra studied her son. He'd become a tall, good-looking man. But earlier when she'd asked them about friends at school, he'd said he was too busy studying and playing football to make any friends. His being anti-social bothered her. And the way

Mia watched him had Shandra wondering what she knew that he wasn't telling. Had he and Holly been more than acquaintances?

Ryan returned to the great room in his snow pants and heavy coat. A stocking cap pulled down over his ears.

"I thought you were just getting the sled ready to get the tree. You're both dressed as if we're going to get the tree today." Shandra shoved the blanket off her lap.

"We might want to try a few runs on the hill after we make sure the sled is fully functioning." Ryan winked at Jayden.

"Oh no, you don't!" Mia hopped off the couch. "You're not going sledding without me." She ran down the hall to her bedroom.

Ryan held out a hand to Shandra. "What about you? Care for a ride down the hill?"

She smiled. "I think I'll just stay here and get dinner ready. I hadn't planned on getting a tree until tomorrow and that's when I'll venture out on the mountain with you." She saw the conspiratorial look between the two men she loved. "And don't gang up on Mia."

"What about me?" Mia asked, entering the room dressed in her snowsuit, heavy coat, and stocking cap.

"Don't let them get all the rides down the hill," Shandra said, standing and folding the blanket she'd had wrapped around her.

"I won't. Let's go!" Mia did an about-face and strode down the hallway to the mud room and her boots and gloves. Jayden followed.

"If you're staying behind, do some more internet digging on Nathan and Cindy Garvie, spelled with an 'ie,'" Ryan said, quietly.

"Holly's parents?" Shandra whispered back.

"Yes. And Holly too, if you can. They aren't stand-up citizens and I think Holly was trying to run away from them and possibly this Botts kid." Ryan kissed her forehead. "I'll make sure they have fun."

Shandra smiled. "I think you've been waiting for them to come home so you could go sledding. You know there are a good number of your nieces and nephews you could take sledding when you need a release." She waved her hand at the wall in the great room lined with family photos.

"But these are my kids."

"Are you coming or staying here where it's nice and warm?" Mia taunted.

A grin spread across Ryan's face. "I'm being beckoned."

"Go. Have fun but don't break anything." Shandra smiled at his excitement to go sledding.

"We'll be careful." He strode down the hallway and Shandra wandered into the kitchen to make a cup of tea and grab her laptop. What had Ryan found out about the Garvies that had him suspicious?

Chapter Five

By the time Ryan and the twins returned, Shandra had spent an hour saving information she'd found on both the parents' social media sites. She hadn't found a Skylar Botts anywhere on social media that was male and the right age. Nor did she find any listing for Holly.

She had the milk warming on the stove and homemade enchiladas cooking in the oven.

"It smells wonderful in here!" Mia said, sliding onto a stool minus her outdoor clothing and boots.

"I have milk ready and dinner is in the

oven. All that we need now is a salad and to warm the tortilla chips." Shandra set salad fixings out on the counter.

"I can help with the salad," Jayden said, walking to the sink and washing his hands.

"Thank you. That will give me time to make the hot chocolate." Shandra spooned chocolate into the pan along with sugar and vanilla and stirred. "Where's Ryan?" she asked, not hearing anyone else in the mudroom.

"He's feeding the horses so you don't have to go out later," Mia said with a sparkle in her eye.

"That's thoughtful. But I like visiting the horses." Shandra wondered what Ryan was really doing. He also knew how much she enjoyed feeding the horses in the winter to spend more time with them when there was too much snow to ride.

As she set a cup of hot cocoa in front of the twins, the back door opened and she heard stomping. "Continue what you're doing and I'll go help Ryan."

Mia and Jayden exchanged a look. Mia picked up her drink and sipped, and Jayden continued cutting lettuce.

Shandra hurried down the hallway to the mudroom. She pulled the door closed behind her. "I see why you think the parents may have something to do with Holly's death."

Ryan hung up his coat and faced her. "What did you learn?"

"They seem to be drug users and aren't happy their darling daughter went to college rather than stayed home and supported them."

"How did you find that out?" Ryan sat down and unlaced his boots.

"Cindy posts all her rants on social media. The week that school started for the twins, she posted about how her daughter thought she was better than her parents and was leaving them destitute by going to college." Shandra wrinkled her nose. "Mr. Garvie posts disgusting photos of women barely dressed and makes rude comments.

It's no wonder Skylar scared Holly, he sounds just like her father."

"You added a little more to what I found out going through police channels. Did you learn anything about Holly?"

"Dinners burning!" Mia shouted from the kitchen.

"I think that's our cue to get in the kitchen because they are both old enough to pull something out of the oven." Shandra grinned and spun about, striding down the hall even though she knew there was no rush. Let the kids think she believed them incompetent to pull a casserole out of the oven.

She walked into the kitchen and found the dish of enchiladas on a pad on the island along with sour cream, hot sauce, guacamole she'd made, the salad, and dressings. Mia set the last plate on the island.

"Dinner is ready and we're starved." Mia smiled and took her seat at the island.

Ryan entered the room and they all sat down and filled their plates.

When the twins started dishing seconds, Ryan asked, "Mia, did Holly ever talk about her family?"

Shandra watched intently without looking like she was interested. She hoped the twins didn't feel some loyalty to the dead young woman and kept her secrets.

Mia set down her fork and picked up her glass of milk. She drank slowly before putting the glass down and looking at Ryan. "Not to me. But she did to her roommate. Who is friends with my friend Emma and she said Holly never called or talked to her parents. She had an older sister that she talked to a little bit, but Holly mostly used her phone for texting. Emma said she did it as if she were trying to hide a secret."

Shandra thought about the fact the phone had been taken. Unless it had been thrown out into the snow. Whoever was found with the phone would be considered a suspect.

"Do you have Holly's cell phone number?" Ryan asked.

Mia nodded. She slipped off the stool and headed out of the kitchen.

"Can you find out who she was texting with her cell number?" Jayden asked, not looking up from the second helping of enchilada on his plate.

"Yes, it will take some time, serving subpoenas and warrants to get access to her records. But we'll be able to bring up her text messages and who she called and who called her." Ryan picked up a chip, held it in front of his face, and studied Jayden.

Shandra held her breath. Jayden had the look on his face that he wanted to say something but held back. Was it because Mia's number would be in Holly's phone or his?

Mia walked back into the room with her phone. "Here's her number."

Ryan pulled a piece of paper over to him and grabbed a pen. "Go ahead."

Mia recited the number.

Jayden shook his head. "That's not right." He peered at his twin. "You must have read someone else's number."

Mia held the phone up, facing Jayden. "That is the number."

He shook his head. "That's not the number she used to text me."

"That's why you looked so pensive when Ryan said he could find out all the numbers calling and texting Holly." Shandra felt some relief that Jayden had confessed to having texted with Holly, but it also was one more piece of evidence against him.

Jayden ducked his head. "Holly and I went out a couple of times. She always texted me and said she needed to talk. I listened while we ate a burger or walked."

"You are a good listener when you aren't playing big brother," Mia said, putting a hand on his arm.

"What did you two talk about?" Ryan asked, plucking another chip from the bowl.

"Holly was really confused. She felt like she was being manipulated by her parents and her sister. Her parents aren't good people. She worked almost a forty-hour week while going to high school to pay the rent and buy food because her parents spent all their money on drugs. They played on her sympathies. They told Holly since her sister ran away it was up to her to help them survive."

"That's a lot of pressure to put on a child," Shandra said, disliking the Garvies even more.

"She talked about calling her sister, maybe that's who she had the other phone for?" Jayden's gaze held Ryan's.

"What did she tell you about her sister? Name, where she lives?" Ryan asked.

"Holly said her sister's name was Hannah. I don't know where she lives. Holly never said. But Hannah kept telling her to leave their addict parents and make something of herself. Holly knew she had to do well in high school to get scholarships to break away. And she had a couple of teachers who were helping her. That's how she received a scholarship from WSU, one of her teachers knows someone on the scholarship committee."

Jayden stirred his enchilada. "She said it was harder for her to get away from her parents than her sister. Hannah became pregnant at fifteen and ran off with the father. Holly felt obligated to her parents to help them since Hannah's running off made their habits worse."

"You mean they made her think they couldn't live without her. When they really wanted to keep her a slave to feed their addictions," Shandra said, with more anger than she'd meant.

Mia and Jayden stared at her.

"Sorry. It just makes me angry when parents manipulate their children because they are selfish." Shandra rose and carried her plate to the sink. She had never voiced this before but she'd felt all the adults in Jayden and Mia's lives before they came to live with them had been selfish and that was what caused their deaths and put the burden of remorse on the twins.

A hand rested on her shoulder. Shandra

studied the reflection in the kitchen window. Mia stood, looking over her shoulder.

"Mom, we know what you did for us. We love you for it and know you would never put yourself before us." Mia wrapped her arms around Shandra and hugged her.

Pride and love brought a lump the size of clay she molded for mugs to lodge in her throat. She couldn't speak, just return the hug.

Ryan's chest expanded seeing the two women in his life hugging. He glanced at Jayden. The young man seemed torn between staying where he was and joining the women. After the night they had, he was pretty sure the twins were both in need of a hug. He tapped Jayden's arm and tipped his head toward Mia and Shandra.

Jayden bolted off the stool and wrapped his arms around his sister and mom.

Ryan watched, warmth filling him that he and Shandra had done the right thing when they adopted the two. But now, he had to find the evidence as to who killed Holly

Paty Jager

Garvie so Jayden wasn't the only suspect.

Chapter Six

After dinner, the twins took showers and went to bed early. They'd had a long night without much sleep and played hard while sledding. Shandra snuggled up on the couch under a blanket. Her eyes grew heavy as she listened to Ryan tapping on the keys of his work laptop.

Shandra shaded her eyes with a hand as she peered up the pine tree at the flicker tapping his beak against the brown bark. "Why are you making such a racket?" she asked the bird. It stopped pecking the tree and flew away. Redirecting her gaze to the area around her, she found her grandmother sitting on a blanket, separating cones from the different species of trees.

"Why are you separating the cones, Ella?" Shandra asked.

"To find which one these seeds belong to." Ella opened her hand. Two different-looking seeds lay in the palm of her hand.

"That will take a while. Do you want my help?" Shandra crossed her feet to lower onto the blanket.

"There is more to be gathered. These may not belong to any of the cones I have."

Grandmother dissolved into a mist and left Shandra standing in a forest.

"I think I've found Holly's sister," Ryan's voice filtered into Shandra's consciousness.

She shook off the feeling she should understand the dream and sat up. "Where?"

"Haferville. I think Holly didn't plan on waiting for someone to pick her up. She decided to walk and took the wrong road." Ryan sat on the couch beside her. "She was going to stay with her sister for Christmas break."

"You need to call her sister. If she hasn't had any contact with her parents, she may be waiting for Holly to show up." Shandra sat up feeling the sorrow Hannah would feel when she learned about her sister.

Ryan stood and walked over to the table. He sat down in front of his computer and dialed his cell phone. As many years as he'd been making this type of call, it never got any easier.

"Hello. Is this Hannah Garvie?" he asked when a young woman answered his call.

"Yes, but Hannah Bernal now. Why? Who are you?"

"I'm Sheriff Ryan Greer with the Weippe County Sheriff's Department. I'm sorry to inform you that your sister, Holly, was the victim of a homicide last night."

"No!" she blurted before gathering herself. "When? Where? Cam said Holly must have changed her mind when she didn't show up where she said to meet her."

"Were you and your husband meeting her last night?" Ryan asked.

"No, just Cam. It was too late to take our boys out of bed, so I stayed home. Where did this happen?"

"Where were you to meet Holly?" Ryan asked, wanting answers before he gave out the information the woman was requesting.

"She said she'd be at a diner in Huckleberry around eleven. But Cam said the place was closed and he didn't see anyone sitting in a car waiting. He waited until midnight, then came home figuring she changed her mind or my parents forced her to go there." The hostility rang in Hannah's voice when she mentioned her parents.

"She and her ride were sitting at Rigatoni's, the Italian restaurant. She told her ride that her father was there to pick her up at one A.M. and left the restaurant. An hour later her body was found on County Road Fifteen."

The woman sobbed. "If it was our effing parents who picked her up then you can pretty much arrest them. They must have heard that Holly was coming to see me and stopped her any way they could." Again, the anger in her voice was more than a child who had differences with her parents. What had the two done to her, and possibly Holly, to make her hate them so much?

"They are on my list. Did your sister ever talk to you about Skylar Botts?" Ryan asked.

"Yes. She said he reminded her of our father and made her fear him. He tried grabbing her once when she was walking back from a late lab at the college and she screamed. Some other students came rushing up and the creep ran away."

"Did she say why she thought Botts was interested in her?" Ryan had to find a reason for the young man's attention toward Holly.

"No. She just said she didn't like his attention and had talked to a supervisor but he wasn't any help."

"I have one more question. Did you know your sister had two different cell phones?" He hoped she could shed some light on this.

"Yes, she used one to call our parents and one for everything else."

"You're sure she only used it for calling

your parents?" He wondered why the young woman had used the same phone she called her parents with to meet up with Jayden.

"That would be my guess but I'm not sure. I do know she said she kept the phone that had our parent's number in it in her room and only called them back after they'd left several messages. She didn't like talking to them all the time, it made it harder to concentrate on her school work."

That made sense, Ryan thought. "Again, I'm sorry for your loss. I may need to call you again for clarification on information I turn up."

"That's fine. I want her killer found, even if it is our parents." The call went silent.

Ryan stared ahead at his computer. That was interesting.

"Well, what did she have to say?" Shandra asked.

Ryan returned to the couch and in a quiet voice relayed what he'd learned from Hannah.

Shandra leaned back. "She believes her parents killed her sister. Why?"

"Because they found out Holly was spending Christmas with her." Ryan knew Shandra's mind was whirring with what-ifs. She had proved helpful to many homicide investigations over the years.

"Beforehand Holly had told them to meet her at Ruthie's at eleven? That doesn't make sense. The twins knew that Ruthie's wouldn't be open that late. They wouldn't have told her that was where they could wait for someone." Shandra shook her head. "I think Holly planned to meet someone else all along. Why give her sister the wrong information? Why pretend her father was there to pick her up when she didn't want to go home?"

"I agree, the young woman was deceitful. But why? And who had she been meeting?" Ryan studied his wife. She was trying to piece things together as well.

She shook her head and said, "I just had a dream with Ella. She was sorting coniferous cones and trying to find which cones some seeds came from. But the seeds weren't the same." Her brow furrowed. "As usual she can't seem to give us the straight answer, we have to riddle it out."

Ryan chuckled. It had always amused him that Shandra's grandmother would come to her in dreams but leave cryptic messages. He always wondered if it was because she didn't know the truth either and just went with what she thought might get them close to the real information or she liked seeing how astute her granddaughter was.

"Let's go to bed. The contents of Holly's dorm room will be in the office waiting for me tomorrow and with luck an autopsy report." Ryan stood.

"You promised to go with us to get the tree tomorrow," Shandra stood, folding the blanket.

"I'll leave for Warner early and be back by noon, one at the latest. That will give us enough daylight to find the perfect tree and bring it home." He walked over and turned off the lights, before putting his arm around Shandra's shoulders and walking beside her to their room. This was supposed to be a

Christmas Chaos
wonderful family Christmas. So far it had
been full of fear, angst, and suspicions.

Chapter Seven

The next morning after Ryan headed to Warner, Shandra and the twins walked out to the corrals to feed the horses.

"Remember at our adoption when Lil gave us Cookie and Cream?" Mia said, leaning against the fence, petting the nose of her mare Glitter, the horse she'd received when she'd outgrown her pony, Cookie.

"That was the first time we'd ever been given such a big gift," Jayden said, his voice holding awe. He stood by the fence rubbing up and down the wide blaze on his gelding's face. "Then you and Dad gave us these two." Jayden shifted his gaze from his horse to Shandra.

"You'd outgrown the ponies, and if we wanted you to go on rides with us you needed a horse." Shandra smiled at her kids. "They will always be here when you come home and if you end up someplace where you can keep them, you may take them with you."

Mia flew toward Shandra and hugged her. "I know it's wrong but I wish you had been our mother from the beginning."

Shandra smoothed Mia's hair and kissed her temple. "Some people aren't parent material. You can't fault your biological mother for that or the fact your aunt didn't really know what she was getting into by pretending to be your mom." The biggest fault lay with their father, but she would never say that. The twins adored their father because he had been their shelter in a turbulent childhood.

Jayden turned from the corral and stared at the barn. "Do you think it would be strange for someone like me who has had a less-than-ideal childhood to become a therapist?"

This was good news to Shandra. "I think it would be helpful to you, and with your past, you may be able to help children who have gone through similar experiences because you have something in common."

Jayden smiled. "I'll talk to my counselor when I get back and switch my major. I could be helpful to law enforcement by talking to people."

"Yes, you could." Shandra pulled him into a hug. "I see the two of you doing wonderful things in the future."

Shandra released him and said, "Let's go in and bake some cookies. All the Greers will be here for Christmas day, and Lil and Claude will be here for Christmas Eve. She didn't want to share you with the Greers."

The twins laughed and followed Shandra into the house. She was happy to have them back and hoped they could discover who killed Holly by Christmas. Which was in ten days.

~*~

Ryan entered the Sheriff's Office and discovered reports of a car pileup on Highway 90, an attempted break-in outside of Warner, and three drunk drivers brought in. It had been a busy night while he was at home enjoying time with his family. He dealt with the reports and caught up with his new Patrol Captain, Gerald Speaks. Gerald and Ron had been the deputies when he was a detective. Now they had both moved up. Ron as the new detective and they had two new deputies Shirl Croft and Bud Hartsell. Everyone had to do patrols and take care of the county but when something like a homicide came up, it was also everyone helping to solve it.

"Gerald, I didn't see any reports come through on the Garvie homicide. Did you hear anything?" Ryan asked.

His patrol captain and friend of over a decade didn't meet his gaze. "State Police took over the investigation since your kids are involved."

Ryan glared at his captain. He knew Gerald had nothing to do with it, but he was the person standing in front of him. "How the hell did they get wind of the homicide and that Jayden and Mia were witnesses?"

Gerald cleared his throat. "Bud was on an open frequency when he requested assistance with a homicide. Ron got there straight away, but a Stater came by also and listed the names of those involved. It must have caught the attention of his supervisor."

"How can we keep the kids' names out of this and not stir up the past if the State Police are working the case? And if they are, why haven't they contacted us?" He stared at Gerald. "Sorry, I didn't mean to blast you. I'll go have a talk with the person in charge of the investigation."

Ryan retreated to his office and called his contact in the Idaho State Police. He knew it was protocol for the State to take over when a county law enforcement officer or their family was involved in a crime, but this wouldn't do. He didn't want what happened over ten years ago to be brought back up. The twins had been doing so well, he didn't want anything to make them slide backward.

"ISP Detective Decker."

"James, it's Ryan Greer. I just heard you took over the Garvie Homicide." Ryan kept his tone conversational when he felt anything but.

"Ryan, I figured I'd be getting a call from you. Yeah, you know the drill, when an officer is related to persons of interest, whether they are suspects or witnesses, the findings could be compromised."

"Hold on. Jayden and Mia aren't suspects. They are witnesses after the fact." Ryan wasn't going to have only his kids looked at as the suspects. "The victim's parents are likely suspects, as well as another college student who had been harassing the victim."

"That is why this case was given to us. You can't remain impartial when it's your kids who are involved."

"James, come question them. They had nothing to do with the homicide. They just gave another student a ride to Huckleberry." Ryan was already formulating in his mind the next steps he'd take to get his hands on the autopsy and forensics. Also, the victim's belongings from her dorm room.

"I was just getting ready to call and set up a time to question them at the Huckleberry Police Station. Ryan, stay out of this. It will go better for your kids." The line went silent.

"Stay out my ass!" Ryan had never felt so useless to his family as he did right now. He held his head in his hands while he thought. There hadn't been any message about the dorm room contents. He buzzed the front.

"What do you want little brother?" Cathleen asked. She only called him sheriff when they were around other people. On the phone, she kept him humble.

"Did anyone send the notice to the WSU security that we needed the contents of Holly Garvie's room?'"

Cathleen let out a breath. "No. I forgot to call them back when I was put on hold."

His day was looking up. "Good! I'll go get it myself. Call Shandra and tell her I'll be late and we'll get the tree tomorrow. This is more important."

"Don't step on any State Trooper's toes. I was here when they came in and took away all the reports on this homicide. How are the twins holding up?" Cathleen's voice took on the husky mother-bear tone she used when someone had crossed her family.

"So far okay. But if the State Police let their names out, I don't know how they will respond."

"Don't worry. Mom and Dad are taking care of that. They invited Til and Jasper over for dinner tonight." Cathleen ended the call.

Ryan grabbed his hat and headed out of the building, smiling. Til and Jasper Miller owned all of the newspapers and radio stations in the upper half of Idaho. He had no doubt his mom and dad would make sure the Millers didn't print their grandchildren's names in any of their media.

Shandra walked into the bedroom when she saw it was Cathleen calling. "Hi Cathleen, what's up?"

"Ryan wanted me to let you know he won't be home until late tonight."

Something must be wrong. "Why will he be late? Does it have something to do with the homicide?" Shandra asked.

"Yes. The State Police have taken over the homicide because of the twins being involved."

"They didn't kill that poor girl!" Shandra said, becoming frustrated.

"I know that, but you know Ryan can't be involved because of his connection. It's like when you and he were dating and your ex-boyfriend ended up dead at the ski resort. That was given to the State Police too. It will be fine."

"If Ryan is off the case, why won't he be home at noon like he said?" Shandra knew Ryan wouldn't quit investigating even though it wasn't legally his case.

"The call to the college security didn't get made asking them to gather up the victim's effects in her room. He went to Pullman to get them before the State Police think of it." There was a smile in the tone of Cathleen's voice.

"Good. That may help. Thank you for the call. See you at Christmas Mass if not before." Shandra ended the call and walked into the great room.

Jayden stood in the middle of the room holding his phone and watching his sister.

"What's wrong?" Shandra asked.

"That was a Detective Decker with the Idaho State Police. He wants Mia and I to be at the Huckleberry Police Station at one this afternoon. He said he is taking over the Garvie homicide. Why?" The fear and confusion on Jayden's face took Shandra across the room to put an arm around his waist.

"That was Aunt Cathleen, she said the

State Police have taken over the case because of your connection to Ryan."

"What about getting the tree this afternoon?" Mia asked, her large brown eyes reminded Shandra of a deer that had been startled.

"Ryan can't make it. He's working on the case without authority." Shandra smiled at the two. "But you don't want to tell the State Police that."

Jayden and Mia nodded, but they didn't seem to be any less frightened.

"Don't worry. I'll be right there with you when you talk to the detective. All you have to do is tell the truth and you'll be fine. They probably think Ryan didn't ask you enough questions since he is your dad." She hoped that was true and she and Ryan could get this settled before the word got out that the Woodcock children were involved in another murder.

Chapter Eight

Ryan used his uniform and badge to get campus security to open Holly Garvie's dorm room.

"Could you find someone who can tell me which side of the room is Holly's? There doesn't seem to be any photos on either side to help me make the decision. Or I could just go through a desk and see what I find." Ryan knew the security guard wouldn't go for that invasion of privacy.

The man in his forties, with body-building muscles, talked into his cell phone. "Someone will be here shortly."

"Thank you," Ryan said, placing the

three plastic totes he'd brought with him to gather the victim's things on a chair by a desk. If the security guard hadn't been in the room with him, he would have started going through the desk. But it wouldn't look good if he rifled through the desk not belonging to the victim.

Ten minutes later, a young woman with brown hair, green eyes, and large glasses, walked into the room wearing a sweatshirt and jeans. "What's going on?" the young woman asked.

"I'm Ryan Greer, Sheriff of Weippe County in Idaho. And you are?"

"I'm Rory Haston, resident staff for this floor of the dorm. What do you want with me?" The young woman's gaze flashed around the room.

"I need to know which side of the room is Holly Garvie's." Ryan motioned to the totes.

"Why? What are the totes for? Did something happen to Holly?" As Ms. Haston asked the questions her voice grew shriller.

"I'm sorry to inform you that Holly Garvie was a victim of a homicide two nights ago." Ryan watched the young woman. Her eyes widened and her head shook slightly as she took in what he'd said.

"Holly's dead? It can't be. She was only going to her sister's for Christmas. Was it the twins she was riding with? Did they get in a car accident?" Ms. Halston went from fearful to angry in a flash.

"It wasn't a car accident. Jayden and Mia had nothing to do with what happened." He turned the tables on the woman. "Were you and Holly close? You seem to know a lot about where she was going and how she was traveling."

The woman stared at him, her mouth partially open. She snapped her mouth shut and pointed to the side where Ryan had set the totes. "That side of the room. Do you want help?" she offered.

"No, that's all for now. I'll come talk to you after I have her things boxed up." Ryan turned, dismissing the woman. When he looked up from pulling the totes apart, Ms. Halston was hanging around outside the open door.

"Please close the door," he said to the security guard still standing in the room.

The door shut, and Ryan began going through Holly's desk. He found a bundle of letters. They were all addressed from her sister in Haferville. He put those in the tote. He added all the notebooks, pieces of paper, and what looked like a diary or journal. He'd read through all of it when he had it back in Huckleberry.

After cleaning out the desk, he went to the bed that sat up high with storage space underneath and a small chest of drawers. He put everything small that he found in the tote and looked under the bed and mattress. Lifting the mattress, he discovered a phone in the middle of the bed. With that bagged and documented, he put the phone in the tote.

From there he cleaned out all the clothes, shoes, and boxes in the small closet and the drawers under the sink.

"What about the rest of the stuff?" the security guard asked, motioning to the empty suitcases, laundry basket, and other housekeeping items Ryan left.

"If her family doesn't want them, you can give it to another student." Ryan stacked the totes one on top of the other.

The guard took two of the totes from Ryan and led the way down the hall to the elevator.

As they passed a room with the door slightly ajar, the guard pointed his elbow at it. "That's where Rory lives."

"Thanks." They carried the totes out to Ryan's vehicle and deposited them inside. "I'm going back in to talk to Ms. Haston. Do you want to come?" Ryan asked.

The guard shook his head. "I just had to make sure you didn't touch the other student's things. You can talk to Hasty all you want." The man grinned for the first time since they met. "I'll use my card to get you on the elevator. After that, you're on your own."

Hasty. Interesting name, Ryan thought as he followed the security guard back into Regents Residential Hall and stepped into the elevator when the doors opened.

~*~

Shandra drove the twins to Huckleberry and sat with them as they waited for Detective Decker to arrive.

"What do you think he wants to ask us?" Mia asked in a whisper.

"Probably the same things Ryan asked," Shandra said, smiling. She also wondered why the ISP Detective wanted to question them again. Most likely because it was their dad who questioned them the first time. "I'm sure it's protocol since a family member was part of the investigation."

The door to the police station opened and a man walked through the door. Shandra barely recognized ISP James Decker in civilian clothes.

"Ms. Higheagle, wish we were meeting again under better circumstances." His gaze lingered a moment before taking in Jayden and Mia.

"It's Mrs. Greer now, and these are Ryan and my children. Jayden and Mia. I understand you wish to talk to them. I will be present when you do."

Detective Decker jerked his attention back to her. "I'm not accusing them of anything, just clearing up some details."

"I will sit in on all conversations you have with them." Shandra stood. "Are you doing this together or separate?"

He studied her. "I'd like to talk to each one alone."

"Fine, Jayden do you mind if your sister goes first?" Shandra asked, knowing he would be happy to let her get it over with.

"I'm okay. I'll just hang out here and play a game on my phone." He pulled his phone out of his pocket.

Shandra motioned for Mia to stand. "Let's go."

Detective Decker led the way to the rooms down the hall past the dispatcher. It was a young man. Hazel, who had worked as the dispatcher even after retiring, was now living in Oregon with her daughter.

Detective Decker stopped at a room Shandra knew well. She'd been inside many times while Ryan questioned witnesses and suspects. She put a hand on Mia's arm and drew her to the side of the table away from the door. She'd been on this side of the table a few times over the years as well.

They settled in chairs and the detective placed the folder he'd been holding on the table in front of him. "I'm recording this as I don't write fast enough. When I turn the recorder on, please state your full name and Shandra as the parent, please also state your name and relationship to Mia."

With that done, the detective asked, "Tell me how you and your brother came to give Ms. Garvie a ride?"

Shandra listened as Mia told Detective Decker everything just as she had told Ryan. This time she didn't stop and ask questions, she just said, Holly asked for a ride, they gave her one to Rigatoni's where they waited for her family to pick her up. She got a text and said her ride was there and left. After they'd finished their desserts and used the restrooms, they'd headed home and found Holly.

Mia swallowed a couple of times before she continued. She told of seeing the hand move in the car lights, recognizing Holly's coat, and then getting out and seeing…Mia stopped, swallowed several times, and said, "If it hadn't been for the coat and purse, I wouldn't have recognized her."

Shandra sat up. "That was the only reason you believe it was Holly? Her coat and purse? What about hair, boots, other clothing?"

"Ms.—"

Shandra glared at him. "Call me Shandra. This is something Mia didn't say before. Has anyone checked the dental records or DNA to make sure the dead young woman is Holly?"

"As you just stated, we didn't know

there was a possibility it wasn't until just now like you." Detective Decker shifted his attention to Mia. "Can you think of anything else?"

Mia shook her head.

"Thank you. I'll have your statement typed up so you can sign it before you leave today. Right now, you can change places with your brother."

Shandra nodded and remained seated. As soon as Mia stepped out the door, she said, "From what I've gathered from the kids, Holly was a loner without a loving family. She might have found someone to help her escape everything she wanted to be rid of." And she had a feeling that person was Skylar Botts.

Chapter Nine

Ryan knocked on the slightly ajar door of Ms. Haston's room.

"Come in!" she called out.

Entering, Ryan noted the room was the same size as the one Holly shared, but it had one bed, its own bathroom, and a kitchenette.

Rory sat at the desk. Her computer monitor showed a social media site.

"I hope you aren't spreading the word about Holly's death," Ryan said, opening his notebook.

She spun from the desk and glared at him. "I didn't invade her privacy in life, why would I do it in death?"

"Just making sure. It's easier to catch who did this if the truth doesn't get distorted by rumor." Ryan grabbed a stool and sat in front of the young woman. "What can you tell me about Holly Garvie? Who were her friends? What did she like to do?"

"Why are you asking me?" Rory asked in a confrontational tone.

"You are in charge of the young women on this floor of the dorm. You should see who they hang out with and what they do when they aren't in classes." Ryan wondered why she was being uncooperative.

"She only really talked to and hung out with her roommate, Sybil Krill. She went home to Eureka, California for the holiday. I took her to the Spokane airport the day before Holly left with the twins."

"Do you happen to have Ms. Krill's phone number?" Ryan asked.

"Yeah, she was going to text me when she needed a ride from the airport when she came back." Ms. Haston spun around and picked up her cell phone. She recited the number and put the phone back down, before facing Ryan.

"What did Holly do when she wasn't in class?" Ryan asked.

Ms. Haston shrugged. "She was in the library a lot. I'd see her sitting outside by herself most Sundays when everyone else was either at church or still sleeping."

"What degree was she studying for?"

"I'm pretty sure it was nursing. The night that damn Skylar grabbed her she was coming from a lab in the nursing department." The young woman's face darkened and her eyes glared.

"Tell me about Skylar Botts. What do you know about him?" Ryan felt confident by Rory's reactions she knew the young man.

"He isn't a student. He walks around the campus like he is, but he's a night janitor. He's supposed to work in the male dorms but he wanders wherever he pleases and harasses the girls. I've caught him loitering down in the main commons area of this building. He can't get up the elevator without a resident card. Only the people who live in the building have a card." Rory crossed her arms. "When I see him loitering, I call security. They haul him off but they don't fire him or put a restraining order on him. He's going to do more than grab someone one of these days. He's a pervert who should be locked up."

"I can't do anything about that. It's not my jurisdiction. Where could I find Skylar now? Are they doing maintenance while the school is closed for the holidays?"

"Yes, they are doing maintenance, but I haven't seen Skylar since the day Holly left."

Jayden sat in the chair beside Shandra when he entered the room. Crossing his arms, he gave Detective Decker his sullen, I don't give a crap stare.

Shandra put a hand on the arm closest to her and squeezed. She knew he was more upset by the whole mess than his sister but he would never let anyone know. He was the same way when she and Ryan found the two at night in the forest. He'd not said much and kept the fact he'd seen his father and aunt shortly after they'd been killed.

They went through giving their names for the recording and began the interview.

"Jayden, I'll ask you the same thing I asked your sister," Detective Decker said. "Tell me about the day and night of Holly Garvie's death."

The words came slow and measured from Jayden. Shandra felt as if he were determining how each word would sound before he said it. Why would he worry about that?

He repeated what Mia had said, in his own words. Only he didn't bring up the coat other than Mia saying it looked like Holly's coat. "Her face and head had been smashed as if someone had used a sledgehammer," he said, just as he'd said it when Ron came on the scene and when Ryan questioned him.

Shandra thought back. Had they told Jayden an axe had been found with Holly's blood and hair on it?

"Why do you say it looked like she'd been hit by a sledgehammer?" Detective Decker asked.

Jayden stared across the table. His gaze not wavering. "Because of how it was crushed in sections and Mia said it looked like that's what happened." Jayden shuddered and Shandra caught his hand, giving it a squeeze.

"Have you seen a skull crushed by a sledgehammer before?" the detective asked.

"No! But once you see something like that it doesn't ever go out of your mind. The more I see it in my head I see the fragments of bone and white that Mia said was brain matter. It's something you can't unsee. Instead of letting it haunt me, I try to figure out what could have caused it and why someone would do it."

Shandra smiled at Jayden and then the detective. "Jayden is planning to be a therapist."

Detective Decker continued to study Jayden. He appeared to want to say or ask something else but was unsure how to say it.

"If you have nothing else to ask, we'll be leaving." Shandra stood.

The detective waved her back into her chair. "The victim's phone was missing. Did you see her with it prior to her leaving the restaurant?"

Jayden's body slumped a little as if he relaxed. "Yes. She kept texting someone and then said, her ride was there. When she left the restaurant, her phone was in her hand."

"Do you know who she was texting?"

"No. She was across the table from Mia and I. She barely said anything the whole drive and while we waited with her." Jayden stopped as if thinking. "Holly tried to tell us to go on home. She said she could wait alone. Mia insisted we wait to make sure someone did arrive." He glanced at Shandra. "You taught us that. Never leave a person waiting alone."

She smiled. They had turned out to be great kids.

"You think she had other plans and that's why she didn't want you to stay with her?" Detective Decker asked.

"That could be why she was on her phone so much while we sat there. Probably telling whoever picked her up not to come into the restaurant." Jayden perked up for the first time since walking into the Huckleberry Police Station. "Do you think she wasn't going home or to her sister's but hanging out with someone else?"

Shandra faced Jayden. "What do you think? You said she asked you for advice a couple of times."

The detective straightened. "Were you and the victim friends?"

Jayden shook his head. "I wouldn't call it friends. Mia asked me to play decoy so a disgusting guy who was hitting on Holly would leave her alone. So we went to a diner one time and walked around a park the other. Both times she just kind of talked about her dysfunctional family and how getting away to college was how she planned to get as far from her parents and her past as she could." He shrugged. "I could kind of sympathize having had a dysfunctional family before Ryan and Shandra adopted us."

"Did you think of her as a girlfriend?" Detective Decker asked.

Jayden frowned. "She was a girl and was an acquaintance, no not a friend. And not a girlfriend as in we liked each other that way. I was just doing my sister a favor and trying to help Holly."

"Your sister a favor? She didn't say anything about being friends with the victim." Now it was the detective's turn to frown.

"They weren't really friends. Holly was in some of Mia's classes. That's how they met. It was after one of those classes that Holly was grabbed by the guy. It was after that that Mia came up with me pretending to date Holly to get the guy to leave her alone."

Jayden leaned back in his chair. "No guy has the right to grab any girl he wants. It's not right. I was just trying to help."

"What is the name of the guy?" Detective Decker asked.

"Skylar Botts. And you'll learn he attacked me after a football practice but I didn't lay a hand on him. My teammates gave him a good beating though." Jayden crossed his arms again, closing himself off to the detective.

Shandra put a hand on his arm. "That's all Jayden has to tell you. We'll be going now." She stood and motioned for Jayden to rise.

"Thank you for coming in. If I have any more questions, I'll give you a call." Detective Decker turned off the recorder and also stood. "Come back in about an hour and you and your sister can sign the printed statement.

Shandra hoped this was the last time she had to visit a police station with the twins.

Chapter Ten

Shandra and the twins walked to Ruthie's Diner after they left the police station. The smell of greasy burgers and fries started Shandra's stomach growling when they stepped through the door.

"My favorite people," Ruthie said, walking forward and giving the twins a hug. Ruthie was Shandra's dearest friend. They had been through a lot together and came through with a stronger friendship.

"Where's Donnie?" Mia asked. She'd babysat for Ruthie and Maxwell's son when she was in high school.

"You big college kids may be out of

school but he still has another week before he gets Christmas break." Ruthie led them to Shandra's favorite booth. "Will Ryan be joining you?"

"No, it's just the three of us," Shandra said, glancing at her phone to see if any messages had been left while she was in the interview room. She'd left her phone on silent to not interrupt the detective and so she wouldn't have to hide what she knew about Ryan. Nothing from him.

"We're here for an early dinner," Shandra said, lowering to the bench seat.

Mia and Jayden sat in the booth across from her.

"So we need caramel, strawberry, and chocolate shakes to start with?" Ruthie asked, smiling at each of them as she said their favorite flavor.

"Carmel for me," Shandra said.

"I'll take the chocolate." Mia raised her hand.

Jayden frowned. "I think I'll have a root beer float. I can get a strawberry shake any time, but I haven't found any root beer floats in Pullman."

Ruthie grinned and said, "I'll let you decide what you want to eat while I get those all started."

Mia's grin stretched across her face. "When I was packing to go to college, I didn't think I'd miss Huckleberry that much. But being back here, I realize I did miss it."

Jayden shook his head. "It's not Huckleberry. It's the people. Friends."

"Something you could do more about accumulating," Mia said, bumping her shoulder against her brother's arm.

Shandra leaned forward over the table and asked quietly, "Jayden, your sister said the only reason she knew the body on the road was Holly's was because of her coat. Both of you think. Was she wearing the same clothes? Did Holly have on any jewelry when you picked her up while she was sitting in the restaurant with you?"

The twins stared at Shandra.

"Are you thinking that poor girl on the

road isn't Holly?" Mia asked in a whisper.

"I think Ryan needs to make sure the State Police do a DNA test or fingerprints if Holly is in the system." Shandra worried that the young woman with the smashed in face had become a casualty of Holly's need to get away from her family and Skylar Botts.

~*~

Ryan finished with Ms. Haston and headed back to Huckleberry. He'd have Shandra go over the items he'd found in Ms. Garvie's room then have them delivered to James at the State Police office.

His phone rang. He hit the answer button on his dash and smiled.

"Ryan, do you have any idea what time you'll get home?" Shandra asked.

"Seven, eight at the latest. Why?"

"We were just trying to decide if we needed to hurry home or could do a little shopping. The kids gave their statements to Detective Decker this afternoon and we had an early dinner at Ruthie's."

"How did the interviews go?" Ryan wished he could have been there but Shandra was better, she wouldn't get tweaked out of shape if Decker was out of line, like Ryan would have.

"Good. But Mia said something that has me wondering if the dead person is Holly Garvie. I think my exclaiming 'the only way you knew it was Holly was because of her coat!' got the detective thinking along those lines."

That was what he loved about his wife. "Good catch. I hope James follows up on that. I'll see if we have a way to check as well. I plan on spending all day tomorrow with all of you. That is if I can get some donuts someplace."

"Don't worry about it. We grabbed a dozen before we went to the police station. We're covered for tomorrow. Just hurry home safe." The call ended.

Ryan smiled. Shandra was the best thing that happened in his life. The twins came in second to that. His phone buzzed. It was rare his dad called him but it was what the caller ID showed him.

"Dad, is something wrong?" Ryan answered.

"Just thought I'd let you know that your mother and I are having the Millers over for dinner tonight. We'll make sure nothing about the twins is put in any of their news channels. And the most important thing. I found your Christmas present for Shandra. We'll keep it until we come over Christmas Day."

Ryan was glad his parents were good friends with the Millers and had enough influence to keep Jayden and Mia's names out of the news. "Thank you for talking to the Millers. What did you find for me to give to Shandra for Christmas?"

"Don't worry about it. Just know you can focus on getting to the truth behind the young woman's death and not have to shop for a gift for your wife."

His dad ended the call. Now he wondered what on earth his dad could have found for Shandra's Christmas present.

He dialed Stu.

"Detective Whorter."

"Stu, it's Ryan. Did forensics pull any fingerprints off Jayden's car that weren't the twins?"

"Yeah, there were three sets of prints. The ones in the back seat didn't match your kids."

Ryan smiled. "See if they match the body's fingerprints."

"You think the young woman with her head bashed in wasn't Holly Garvie?" Stu asked.

"It's a hunch. And if anyone from the state police calls wondering about Ms. Garvie's things from the college, they'll arrive at the station late tomorrow afternoon."

"Copy."

Ryan ended the call and put the radio on a country station for background noise as he ran what they knew over in his head and drove a little over the speed limit to get home sooner. He and Shandra had to go through the totes in his back seat tonight.

Chapter Eleven

Shandra and the twins were just finishing up wrapping the gifts they'd purchased for Lil and Claude when lights illuminated the front windows.

"That should be Ryan. Good thing we wrapped your gift to him first," Shandra said as Jayden carried the presents over by the fireplace, and Mia wound curling ribbon back onto a spool. Saphire had been let in when they came home and had been playing with the ribbon in between getting pets and hugs from Mia.

"Did you tell him we got the donuts?" Mia asked.

"Yes, when he called earlier, I told him we'd picked them up. I didn't want him to have any excuses for going to town tomorrow." Shandra grinned and put the tea kettle on to boil. They could all use a nice chamomile tea to sip as they relaxed before bed.

Pounding on the back door sent Jayden jogging down the hall.

Shandra wondered what her husband brought home that was so big he couldn't open the door.

Jayden returned carrying two tote bins and Ryan followed behind with one.

Shandra walked out of the kitchen. "Is that—"

"Boxes you and I need to go through. I don't want anyone to know about this and especially don't want Jayden or Mia touching anything," Ryan cut her off.

Mia walked towards the table. "Is that Holly's stuff from her room?"

Ryan nodded. "I don't want either of you to touch anything inside the boxes. Even if you were in her room and might have touched something before. There is no sense in adding more fingerprints." He took off his coat and settled it over the back of his chair.

"Once you two get your tea, why don't you go watch a movie in Jayden's room," Shandra suggested to keep their minds occupied while she and Ryan dug through the totes.

"Isn't this, well, something you could get in trouble for?" Jayden asked.

Ryan straightened. "It is. But it's worth it if we can find something in here to tell us what Holly was up to."

"Wouldn't the State Police find it if they had this?" Jayden waved his hand toward the totes.

"I would like to think they would. But they may not be looking as hard for the killer as we are," Ryan said.

Mia gasped. "Did that detective think we killed her?"

"I haven't heard one way or the other, but we know you are innocent and we will find the information that will help the detective prove it." Ryan put an arm around Mia. "There's nothing to worry about. Grab your tea and go watch a movie. If we have questions, we'll come ask you." He released her after kissing the top of her head.

Shandra handed mugs of tea and a plate of cookies to the kids and watched them shuffle down the hall to Jayden's room and close the door. Her heart went out to the two. They had been through more than enough in their short lives. She faced Ryan. "Do you really think we'll find something in there to prove the twins had nothing to do with it?"

Ryan shrugged. "I'm hoping. The dorm resident seemed to know quite a bit about Holly but didn't give up much. I'll ask Mia about her tomorrow. She did have a lot to say about Skylar. He isn't a student. He works at the college. I do believe we need to send a letter of complaint to the Dean and get Skylar removed from the college with all that Mia and Rory told me. That is if he isn't the murderer."

Shandra studied her husband. "Is that who you think did it?"

"I don't know. But he seemed to be infatuated with Holly and likes scaring or trying to get close to the women." Ryan nodded to the two cups on a tray with a plate of cookies. "Bring that into the dining room. We'll work at the table."

Shandra picked up the tray in front of her and followed him.

The three totes sat on the table. "Should I just pick one and start going through it?" she asked.

"Take the one on the end. It was from her desk. I'm going to check out the phone I found under the mattress." Ryan opened the tote farthest from Shandra and pulled out an evidence bag.

"What about leaving our fingerprints?" Shandra held up her hands.

Ryan tugged two sets of latex gloves out of his back pocket. "I thought of that." He tossed a pair over to her.

Shandra donned the gloves and opened the tote. On top was a journal. She smiled. That's why he wanted her to go through this tote. Plucking the flowered book from the top of the contents in the plastic tub, she sat down and opened it to the beginning.

Holly Garvie was written in bold letters on the inside page along with January 1 of this year. It appeared the young woman kept a journal for every year of her life. Shandra wondered if there was any chance they could get a hold of the ones she'd written while growing up. Shoving that thought to the side, she began reading.

As she'd expected the young woman had led a life of work, school, and ridicule by her parents. Shandra's heart ached for Holly. The life she'd left to go to college was harder than college. She came to the end of August and Holly moved to the college. From the wording and lots of exclamation marks, it was evident she was excited to be away from home and moving up in the world.

The journal had shorter passages as her classes became her focus. But she did mention all the times Skylar Botts confronted her. Holly's description of the man made Shandra's stomach churn. Holly even mentioned the man reminded her of her father. Someone she detested. She made a comment about meeting her first twins and that the girl was nice but too talkative and the brother was handsome but aloof. Though later on she mentioned meeting 'the boy twin' for a burger and going for a walk in the park. After both meetings, she put a question mark. Shandra wondered what that was about.

There was also a mention of someone whom she drew a heart for instead of a name when she talked about them. Could this be the person she was really meeting? If so, why had he bashed her head in? Was it a one-sided love?

Shandra looked up from the journal. "Have you found anything interesting on the phone?" she asked Ryan.

"There are only two numbers in this phone. Her parents and Jayden's." Ryan's brow was furrowed deeper than the coils on a vase she'd made recently.

"What do you think that means? Jayden's number being on there?" Shandra didn't like the fact their son's name was on the murdered young woman's phone. The one she rarely used. "How many times did they communicate?"

"It looks like three times. They were meet-ups just like Jayden said." Ryan studied the phone. "If I had parents like Holly's I would have stayed in the Army and put in for stations as far from Idaho as I could get. The nasty remarks and insinuations show no regard for their daughter."

"Her comments about them while she was still living at home this year are so mixed up. One minute she wishes she weren't their child and the next they pile on the guilt and make her sorry she feels the need to run away." Shandra flipped back to a page from March and read the entry to herself.

"I can see why she worked so hard to get a scholarship and go to college," Ryan commented.

Shandra flipped back to where she'd left off in the journal. It was dated around Thanksgiving. The twins had stayed in Pullman for Thanksgiving because Jayden had a game and practice. She and Ryan had run up and taken them to dinner on Thanksgiving Day and watched the football game the next day.

Holly had also stayed in Pullman that long weekend with the person she denoted with a heart. *We talked it over and I'll keep the baby. ♥ says we can get married at the end of the school year.*

"You need to request the medical examiner to check the victim for pregnancy," Shandra said, watching Ryan put the phone back in the evidence bag.

His head jerked up and his eyes leveled on her. "That says she was pregnant?"

"And planning to marry the father in the summer." Shandra stuck her finger in the book where she'd stopped and pulled a notepad over to start taking notes. "We need to find out who represents the heart she uses when writing about this man."

Ryan had his phone in his hands, texting. "I sent a note to the M.E. to check and see how far along Holly was in her pregnancy. But it's hard to believe she was pregnant when no one seemed to think she had a boyfriend." Ryan rubbed his chin. "Rory, the dorm resident gave me the number of Holly's roommate. I'll see if she knows anything." He scrolled through his phone and dialed.

Shandra opened the journal and continued to read. *I've decided to go to Hannah's for Christmas. I wish* ♥ *could come with me but he has obligations.* A stick figure with a tongue hanging out and a knife in its chest was drawn. This was someone that Holly didn't like. Was it another girl for her boyfriend's affections or was her lover married?

Ryan's voice broke through Shandra's thoughts.

"Ms. Krill, I'm looking into the death of your college roommate." A pause. "Her body was found two nights ago." Another pause as Ryan listened. "No, not in Pullman. She was on a road outside Huckleberry—" He'd been cut off. He frowned. "No, there wasn't a car accident. She told the twins her ride was there and left them in a restaurant. Her body was found on a county road outside of town. What I need to know from you is who was she dating?"

Ryan shook his head, his lips pursed. "That's not what Jayden said. He only saw her twice and they just talked. There wasn't a relationship between them."

Ryan's gaze flicked to the hallway and back to Shandra. "I'm sure you would know who your roommate went out with. Why did she spend so much time at the library?"

He listened and then politely ended the call. He blew out air and stared at Shandra.

"She believes that Jayden and Holly were in a relationship."

Chapter Twelve

Shandra stared at Ryan for several seconds. Shaking her head, she opened the journal to the page where she described the twins. "Does this sound like a way she would write about someone she was in love with?"

Ryan took the book, read the page, and studied her. "Not really, but they could have gone from that stage to her giving him a heart when she talked about him."

Her heart thudded in her chest as her stomach pitched. "Do you really want to pull him out here and demand to know if they were more than friends? If he knew she was pregnant? He'll think we believe he killed her. The state police will think it if they talk to the roommate."

Ryan rubbed the back of his neck, trying to release the tension in his muscles. "We have to ask. Even if it makes him mad. There has to be someone she confided in. If not Jayden then maybe he or Mia can think of someone else."

He walked down the hall with heavy steps. Had Holly known how this would tear Mia and Jayden's family apart by catching a ride with them and taking off with someone? He was sure she hadn't thought she'd end up dead.

Stopping beside the door to Jayden's room, Ryan heard the music track for the movie they were watching. It sounded like one of the Outer space movies they liked so well. He knocked and waited. The sound died and the door opened.

Jayden stood in the open doorway, his eyes questioning.

"I need to come in and have a talk with

you." Ryan motioned to the room.

Jayden backed up and plopped on the bed. "Now what do you need to ask us?"

Ryan felt Shandra's presence before she came into view. She sat down on the bed by Mia.

"We discovered in Holly's journal that she was pregnant and planned to marry the person responsible next summer." Ryan watched Jayden as he spoke. "Did she say anything to you about this during your talks?"

"She did ask me if I thought a child could be a better parent than what they had." Jayden shrugged. "That was after she'd told me a bit about her parents' addictions."

Ryan studied him. Jayden appeared to be telling the truth. He wasn't averting eye contact and seemed to be digging to remember what had been said. "And the two of you were never more than just someone she talked to?"

Jayden's jaw clenched as his gaze narrowed. "If you're asking me if I'm the father of her child, I am not. All we did was talk. Well, she talked, I listened and tried to reply with what I thought were rational answers."

Shandra put a hand on his arm. "We believe you, but her roommate seems to think you and Holly were in a relationship. When the State Police talk to her, they are going to be coming back here to ask you about it."

"If she had a boyfriend and her roommate thinks it was Jayden, where did Holly meet him?" Mia asked.

Ryan remembered what Rory had said about Holly spending a lot of time at the library. "For your nursing classes is a lot of research in the library required?" he asked Mia.

"No. Most of the time is spent in the labs. Why?"

"Your dorm resident said that Holly spent a lot of time in the library." Ryan pulled his phone out and texted James. *The victim spent hours in the library. Ask the college to send you surveillance tapes of the library for a month leading up to Christmas Break.*

This isn't your case. James texted back.

But my son's life is on the line.

Copy.

"What was that about?" Shandra asked.

"I sent Detective Decker a text to request the surveillance tapes from the library." His gaze met Jayden's. "We're going to find out who killed Holly and make sure they have someone else to look at besides you."

Mia walked out of the room and came back in texting on her phone. "My friend Emma's sister works in the library for work study. I'm asking her to see if her sister remembers seeing Holly with anyone in the library."

"That's a wonderful idea," Shandra said, giving Mia a hug when she sat back down on the bed.

"I guess I could text Randy and see if he noticed Holly hanging out with a guy at the library. Randy does a lot of research in the library for Professor Walsh." Jayden walked over to the dresser, picked up his phone, and started texting.

"Don't tell them that Holly is dead," Ryan warned.

"We won't," the twins said in unison.

Shandra smiled at Ryan and stood. "When you get a reply, we'll be out in the dining room going through the rest of Holly's things." She held out a hand and led Ryan out of the bedroom and back to the table.

"I have a little more to read in the journal then I'll go through the rest of the desk items." She opened the journal to where she'd placed a piece of paper and continued reading. There were only a few more entries. They just talked about her apprehension of visiting her sister but elation that she didn't have to go home for the holidays.

Shandra put the journal down and started pulling out the papers and notebooks along with textbooks and a library book in the tote. The papers were mostly school work and some tests. Holly had been an excellent student. Shandra flipped the pages in the notebooks, looking for anything written other than notes or assignments. She didn't find a thing. A box of stationery was missing two envelopes. There were indentions on the empty piece of paper on the pad of stationery. Shandra walked over to her roll-top desk and found a pencil. She shaded the page and read what had been written on the page that had been ripped off the pad.

Dear Hannah,

I am looking forward to visiting you for Christmas. I'm sure it will be much better than what we grew up having for the holidays. Two drunk or high parents never made for a good time. I am catching a ride with a brother and sister who live in Huckleberry. If you could meet me at the diner at 11 P.M. on Wednesday night I'll wait there for you.

Holly

"She did write a letter to her sister saying to meet her at the diner. She doesn't say Ruthie's but it's the only 'diner' in Huckleberry," Shandra said, holding up the page she'd shaded.

"Leave that out of the box. It would be suspicious if James found that. Her sister can confirm a letter was sent." Ryan pulled out another library book from his tote. He held it up by the covers and shook it with the pages flapping downward. A piece of paper drifted to the floor.

"What's that?" Shandra asked, carrying the library book she found over to Ryan.

He bent and picked up the paper.

6 PM north door.

"That's odd," Shandra said. "I wonder which north door and who gave her that?" She held her book as Ryan had and shook. Two pieces of paper floated to the floor. She bent, picked them up, and studied the handwriting. "One good thing, this is not Jayden's handwriting. His you can hardly read." She smiled at Ryan and handed him the two papers.

One paper read; *Can't make tonight.*

The second one read; *We'll talk about it when we meet.*

"This is very sneaky the way they are passing notes. It can't be a student. They would have just met out in the open." Shandra studied Ryan. She could see he was thinking the same thing.

Chapter Thirteen

The next morning after everyone had a big breakfast, Ryan drove to Huckleberry and handed the totes over to Stu to take them to Detective Decker of the State Police.

"Where do you want me to say I got these from?" Stu asked as he closed the back of his SUV.

"You can say I was picking up the victim's belongings when they came for all the information on the case and I handed it over to you as soon as I knew the case was no longer being worked by the county." Ryan knew it was a bit of a lie but James would know that it had been in Ryan's hands at some point.

"You don't think he'll ask you why you didn't hand it over when you talked with him?" Stu asked.

Ryan shrugged. "I don't care what he thinks. I texted him to get a copy of the surveillance tape at the WSU library. The victim may have been meeting up with someone there."

"I don't want to know how you know this." Stu opened his vehicle door and slid in.

"That's probably the best. I won't be in to work today. I already called dispatch and let them know. I promised Shandra and the kids we'd get our Christmas tree today. After what is happening, I don't want to disappoint any of them." Ryan opened the door of his vehicle.

"Enjoy your day with the family." Stu closed his door and drove away.

Ryan sat a moment trying to decide if he should invite Lil to go with them to get the tree. She wasn't getting around as well as she once did. Especially since she and Claude bought a place in town. Best to just have her come Christmas Eve and not trudge around the mountainside.

As he backed out of the parking lot, he spotted Miranda Aducci Porter pulling into a spot at Daily Donut. He could pick up fresh donuts and see if she was working the night the twins and the victim were waiting in her restaurant. Ryan drove down the street and parked across the road from the bakery.

Entering the establishment, his mouth watered. He'd had breakfast but there was something about the aroma of coffee and maple that started his tastebuds salivating. He spotted Miranda. She was tall, curvy, and pretty. Her bubbly personality made her the perfect offspring for the Adducis to leave the care of their restaurant, Rigatonis, as they spent their elder years relaxing.

Miranda turned from the counter a large box of donuts in her hands. "Ryan! I haven't seen you in a long time. I bet you and

Shandra are excited to have the twins home for Christmas." She gave him a one-arm hug and stepped to the side to let him order.

"Do you have a minute?" he said, moving out of line and leading her outside the bakery.

Her smile drooped. "What's happened? Are the twins and Shandra okay?"

"Everyone's fine." He reassured her. "I was just wondering if you were working at the restaurant three nights ago. When the twins and one of their college friends were there?"

Miranda shook her head. "That would have been Wednesday. I don't work nights Sunday through Wednesday. They are the slowest and my manager can take care of things. Here's his number." Miranda pulled out her phone and gave Ryan the number. "Jake should be able to help you."

"Thanks." Ryan smiled at one of his wife's best friends. "How's Alex and the kids?"

Miranda's face lit up. "They are all

doing well. Alex is aging faster than we both like but he'll still be around until the kids are adults. I'm going to call Shandra and invite the family over one night this week. The kids would love to see the twins and Alex is always up for a visit."

"We'd like that. Thanks for the number." Ryan let Miranda go. He could see why his wife had been drawn to Miranda when Shandra had moved to Huckleberry. But for all her good humor, Miranda lived with the threat her husband may not live long. He'd found a way to slow down his death. One that had happened to his father and grandfather, but he hadn't been able to completely stop the process. Luckily, Alex and Miranda had two daughters. Neither of them would have to worry about the disease, it was only carried by the male Porters.

Ryan purchased a new dozen donuts and returned to his vehicle. He dialed the number Miranda had given him.

"Hello?" answered a male voice.

"Jake, this is Sheriff Ryan Greer.

Miranda gave me your number. I have a question about some customers you had in the restaurant Wednesday night."

"Miranda gave you my number?" he said as if he didn't believe it.

"Yes. She and my wife are good friends. I was wondering about the three college kids who sat in a booth by a front window. Do you remember them?" Ryan pushed on.

"Yeah. A guy and two girls. They sure didn't act like they were friends. They all just sat there not saying much. One was constantly texting on her phone. She left first. In a hurry. She barely said bye to the other two. Then about fifteen-twenty minutes later, the other two left. Why are you interested in them?"

"The one that left first ended up a murder victim." Ryan kept his tone neutral.

"She was murdered? Man, I wish I could tell you more. The only reason they stood out to me was because they came in together, and I'd expected laughing and talking and they didn't say a word. Acted as if they barely knew one another."

"Thank you. It corroborates what we learned from the two who remained." Ryan ended the call and headed home.

Shandra dished up the homemade chicken and noodle soup she'd made for lunch and dinner today. At lunch, they would have it with cheese and crackers and for dinner, they would have rolls and salad. It was the easiest meal to keep warm and ready since they would be out all afternoon getting the Christmas tree.

"Dad just arrived," Mia said. She'd been full of excitement all day. While the two had seen a gruesome sight it was obvious other than their knowing the victim and giving her a ride there hadn't been any type of friendship with Holly.

"I'm glad he's back. Randy returned my text about Holly. He knows who she was and did see her a lot at the library." Jayden said, taking his seat at the island.

Ryan walked into the kitchen, kissed

Shandra on the lips, and gave each of the kids a hug. "It looks like the Christmas tree wrangling crew is ready."

"We are, but Jayden and I both heard back from our friends," Mia said, taking her place at the island.

"Did they have anything that would give us a clue to who Holly was seeing?" Ryan asked as his phone buzzed.

Shandra watched him check the number.

He put the phone back and took his seat. "Tell me what you learned."

"Randy said that Holly kept to herself, but would disappear, leaving her books and things sitting on the table, for an hour sometimes. He only knew this because someone always asked who the things belonged to." Jayden was reading from his phone. "But he never saw her with anyone."

Mia held up her phone. "Emma's sister said the same thing. Holly would leave her stuff sitting on a table and disappear through the rows of books. But she saw Holly come out of a back room one time when she was reshelving books. She started toward the room to see if someone was in there when one of the security guards came out of the room."

Shandra asked, "Does Emma's sister know the name of the guard?"

"No. She only knew he was a security guard because he wore the uniform. She'd never seen him before." Mia glanced up. "Do you think this was Holly's boyfriend?"

Ryan stood. "I need to call Decker. This is something conclusive we can have them look into."

Shandra watched as Ryan strode out of the kitchen and into the great room. She shifted her attention to the twins. "Good job, you two. Hopefully, this will be helpful to Detective Decker. Let's eat."

They were sipping their soup when Ryan returned. He sat down but his face was in what Shandra called thought mode.

"Did Detective Decker have anything useful to tell you?" she asked.

Ryan's gaze drifted from Shandra to the kids and back to her. "The victim was pregnant. And they matched the DNA. It was Holly."

"We know that," Mia said.

Shandra responded, "I thought maybe she had changed places with someone after she left you two and that person was killed to make it look like Holly. I thought maybe she and whoever the father of her child was had made it that way so she would be rid of her family."

"The perplexing thing is, Holly was four months pregnant." Ryan peered at each of them. "She conceived before she went to college."

"Then we're looking for someone from where she lived." Shandra feared it would take longer to find the killer if he hadn't been in her life the last three months.

Chapter Fourteen

"The good news is if she was that far along no one can say it's Jayden's," Mia said.

Her brother frowned at her. "As if I would have been that stupid to get someone pregnant. I know how that turns out."

Shandra studied the two. They had been an unwanted pregnancy. At least for the mother. Their father had insisted their mother keep them to term only to turn them over to her older sister and the father. It had turned out that when their father and aunt were killed, their biological mother still didn't want them.

"Let's not think about any of this until after we cut the tree and have it decorated," Shandra said, pulling the two back to the present.

"I agree. This is our family day," Ryan said, finishing his soup. "Let's put the dishes in the sink and suit up."

Ryan and the twins finished their lunch, put their dishes in the sink, and headed to the mud room to put on their warm coats and boots. Shandra set the slow cooker on low and pulled rolls out of the freezer to rise while they played in the snow.

Hunting for the perfect tree was Shandra's favorite Christmas tradition. As a child, she'd gone out with the foreman of her stepfather's ranch and helped pick the tree. If not for the foreman, there wouldn't have even been a Christmas tree in the Malcolm home. Some years her mother and stepfather would go on a trip, leaving her home with the hired hands. But those were usually the best Christmases because they would all try to make her not feel like she'd been left behind. When in truth, the best gift was not having her stepfather around.

Out in the forest with Ryan and Jayden taking turns pulling the sled with Mia riding, they trudged through less than a foot of snow for a good hour. When Shandra rode her horse over the mountain all year long, she would spot trees that she thought would make a good Christmas tree.

Today she'd directed her family to a grove where several fir trees the right height and nicely shaped stood.

"What about this one?" Mia called out, tugging on a limb of a ten-foot tree to shake the snow off.

"That one is nice. But we could go a little taller," Shandra said, pointing to a tree that stood a few feet taller than the rest.

"Did you walk around it to make sure?" Jayden asked, holding up a battery-operated chainsaw.

"I'm getting there," Shandra said, making a circle or as much of one as she could make due to the other trees. "This side doesn't look very good," she said.

"What about this one?" Mia called, standing by a full fir that was off from the rest a bit.

Shandra made her way over a downed log and walked around the tree. She smiled. "I think you picked the perfect one!"

Mia smiled at her brother. "You may cut down this tree."

As the chainsaw echoed through the woods, Shandra, Ryan, and Mia stood back admiring the tree. It fell to the snow with a muffled thump.

Shandra inhaled the scent of pitch and fresh sawdust. When the snow arrived, she'd felt like it was getting close to the holidays, but now, smelling the tree and feeling the brisk air on her face and watching her family carry the tree over to the sled, laughing and joking. This was the holidays.

"I think that was one of our quickest decisions," Ryan said, strapping down the tree.

"It's because I scout for the tree all

year." Shandra pulled out her phone. "Let me get a photo of the three of you pulling the sled." She took the photo and stared at her phone. A thought came to her.

"Now that we know the body is that of Holly Garvie, who has her phone?" Shandra studied her family members.

"The killer," Mia said.

Shandra held her gaze on Ryan. "I think you need to make a call and see if her phone records reveal who she called. He has to be on the list of people who called or were called by her."

"Or I could just call and if he answers tell him I know what he did," Mia said.

"No!" Shandra, Ryan, and Jayden said in unison.

"You'd be putting yourself in danger," Ryan added.

"But he'd have to come here to get me," Mia argued. "If I'm here, and someone we don't know shows up, we'll know he is the killer."

"Not if he sneaks up on you when

you're alone," Jayden said.

Shandra thought about it. Gathering seeds. That's what Grandmother had been doing. They had gathered enough clues to know the person could be anyone from Holly's past. But to find him, they would have to set a trap.

She faced Ryan. "I think it could work. But we won't put it into play until we see if the State Police have exhausted all other means of finding out who the father of her child was."

~*~

Ryan's phone buzzed as he sat in a chair drinking hot chocolate, eating a donut, and watching his wife and kids decorate the tree they'd dragged home and set up in the great room. He glanced at the name. *James Decker*.

He stood and walked into the kitchen before answering.

"James, what have you learned?"

"About as much as you did going through the victim's things. I concluded that your son wasn't her love interest. The library videos do put her in the library a lot but they didn't catch her going into any of the back rooms or catch a security guard coming out of one."

"He might have access to the cameras and turned off the one that would show them meeting. Did you check and see if there were any new hires on the security staff? She had to have gotten pregnant before she went to Pullman. That means she had to have had contact with this person in her hometown." Ryan had been thinking all of this as he watched his family decorate.

"There were no new hires. She could have been knocked up by someone from home and then told her new boyfriend it was his," James cautioned.

"True. Shandra came up with an idea but I want to run it by you first. Mia has the number of the phone that is missing. She could call, or Shandra could call, say she's Mia and tell the person who answers—"

"If they answer. For all we know the

phone has been tossed somewhere," James interrupted.

"True, but this would be one way of finding out," Ryan urged.

"We won't do anything like that unless we can't come up with a suspect."

"Have you brought in Skylar Botts?" Ryan listened to his family laughing and singing Christmas songs in the other room.

"We can't find him. He hasn't shown up for work and his landlord said he thought Skylar had gone home for the holidays. Only Skylar doesn't have any family to go home to."

Ryan stood from where he'd been leaning against the kitchen counter. "He's missing? I'd bet he's the killer and took off. Did he have a vehicle you can put out in a bulletin?"

"I've already done that. No one has seen him. Enjoy the holiday with your family. I'll keep digging into Holly's life before college and see what I can come up with."

The call ended.

Ryan wanted this cleared up before the twins went back to college. They would be known as the two who drove away from the campus with Holly and her ending up murdered. That is what happened, but he wanted someone to take the blame for the act, not his children to be speculated about.

Chapter Fifteen

It was three days until Christmas. Shandra and Mia stood at the kitchen counter decorating cookies while Jayden mixed and baked mini pound cakes. Shandra's heart burst with love and pride. The twins were special people and she was thrilled to be a part of their lives.

Dream a Little Dream, jingled from her phone.

She slid her finger across the screen and tucked the phone between her shoulder and chin. "Are you going to be late for dinner?" she asked Ryan.

"No. I'll be there on time and I'm

bringing someone with me. James."

Shandra flicked a glance at the twins. They were busy, but she could tell they were listening. Their hands had slowed as they continued to decorate and mix.

"I see. For a friendly visit or work-related?" she asked.

"We're going to set Mia's plan into action. From the phone records we believe it could be a married security guard. However, he has an alibi for the time of death. We believe he paid someone to kill her. From the texts they made back and forth, she was pushing him to leave his wife or she would tell her and the dean what had been going on."

"And she thought that would work?" Shandra asked. Here she'd thought the young woman was smart but she'd blackmailed a man who had a lot to lose. Shandra stopped that train of thought. She was a smart person and she'd been pulled into a bad relationship with a professor when she was in college. There were just men out there who used charm to get what they wanted and violence to keep it.

"We'll be there at six." Ryan ended the call.

Shandra remained with the phone tucked on her shoulder as she thought through all that he'd said.

"Mom? What was that about?" Mia asked.

"Ryan is bringing home a guest for dinner. You'll have to finish these cookies by yourself while I start working on dinner." Shandra dropped her phone in an apron pocket and began mixing up a batch of rolls.

~*~

When Ryan entered the house with Detective Decker, Jayden and Mia both became subdued.

"Do you two want to discuss things first or eat first?" Shandra asked.

"Let's eat and I can visit with Jayden and Mia," James said.

The kids looked skeptical but Shandra reassured them with a smile. "Help me carry the food to the dining room," she said.

When she was alone in the kitchen with the twins, Jayden asked, "What is he doing here?"

"Just answer his questions with the best of your knowledge. I think he may want some help catching the killer." Shandra placed a bowl in Jayden's hands and motioned for him to take it into the other room.

"Are they going for my plan?" Mia asked in an excited whisper.

"I'm not sure but they need to catch the man responsible." Shandra handed Mia the basket of rolls.

Shandra entered the dining area and found Mia asking James if they had learned anything new.

He glanced from Ryan to Shandra and back to Mia. "Why would you ask that?"

"Because you are here pretending nothing is going on. That you didn't suspect my brother or me of killing Holly." Mia smiled.

Shandra sat and motioned to the food on the table. "We may as well discuss things as we eat."

Everyone dished up their food and Ryan started the conversation. "Detective Decker has Holly's phone records. She and a security guard at the college were meeting and she texted him quite a bit the last month. She was pushing him to leave his wife for her."

"Which security guard?" Jayden asked.

Ryan glanced at James as if asking permission to give the name. Shandra liked that Ryan was allowing his friend to have control of the situation. James nodded.

"Dean Cotter. Do either of you know him?" Ryan asked.

Mia shook her head but Jayden nodded. "He's the guard that showed up when Skylar jumped me after practice."

Ryan and James exchanged looks.

"Did he ask you why Skylar jumped you?" James asked.

"No, he pulled Skylar off the ground

and escorted him away. The guard never asked me anything." Jayden stared at Ryan. "I saw the same guard another time over by the dorm where Skylar cleaned."

"Do you think he had Skylar following Holly to make her leave the campus?" Mia asked.

"I have a warrant for his phone records but they haven't come in yet. If we can connect him to Skylar, I believe we will find Skylar is the one who murdered the victim," James said, peering around the table.

Mia shuddered. "I could see him bashing in a woman's face."

Shandra put a hand on Mia's arm. She knew what it was like to look into the face of a man who treated women like lower beings.

Dinner ended. Jayden and Mia took the dishes away and prepared dessert.

"Are you sure you want to involve Mia in calling the victim's phone to see if someone has it?" James asked in a quiet voice.

"It's either that or have Jayden call the guard and say he knows all about him and Holly and how the guard used Skylar. That should get a reaction out of the guard. Either he'll come looking for Jayden or he'll go after Skylar," Ryan said.

"If he hasn't killed Skylar already," Shandra added. She'd been involved in enough of Ryan's investigations to know when a killer is trapped, he will go to any lengths to stay out of jail. That included getting rid of everyone he believed knew anything.

"I'd rather put Jayden in this guy's sights than Mia," James said.

Shandra shook her head. "Of the two, Mia is stronger mentally. Jayden sheltered her from their parents' deaths. She isn't as damaged from all of that as Jayden."

"I agree. If she doesn't rouse anyone calling the number, we'll have her contact the security guard and say Holly told her everything. Since the cops aren't leaving her brother alone, she is going to go to the police on Monday." Ryan held Shandra's gaze. "Does that work for you?"

Her heart thudded in her chest. "That means he could come here when we have your family here Christmas day. Are you sure you want that?"

"The more people we have here the less likely it will be for him to think it's a set-up." Ryan smiled. "And for good major, invite the Treats and Porters here for Christmas Eve. Lil's good with a gun but she doesn't move very fast anymore."

Shandra laughed. "Don't you let her hear you say that."

"Who is Lil?" James asked as the twins walked in with Jayden carrying a tray of cupcakes and Mia following with small plates and napkins.

"Those look delicious," Ryan said making a grab for one of the cupcakes.

Jayden swirled the tray away from him. "Mom gets first pick, then our guest."

Shandra smiled at Ryan and plucked the one she knew would be chocolate with a caramel filling. She'd peeked in the kitchen when Jayden was filling the cupcakes.

"While your folks might know what you have there, I don't," James said, his gaze on the tray.

"These are caramel filled, these are chocolate filled and these are lemon filled." Jayden pointed to each grouping of small cakes.

"I like lemon." James took a cupcake with a lemon drop on the top.

Ryan grasped a chocolate-filled one.

Jayden and Mia sat down and each grabbed their favorite flavor.

Finishing his dessert, Ryan took a long drink of milk and cleared his throat. "We've discussed the best way to make this security guard Cotter show his hand."

Chapter Sixteen

Shandra cleared the table and started the dishwasher while Ryan and James went over what Mia would say when she called Holly's phone. Even telling her to leave a message if no one picked up.

Shandra returned to the dining room. Everyone sat around the table as Mia dialed the number and hit speaker. The call went straight to voice mail. She left a message saying she knew whoever had the phone was the person who killed Holly and she was going to inform the police.

"Now what do I do?" Mia asked.

"Now you call this number." James slid

his notepad over to her, tapping a spot on the page. "This time you tell him Holly told you everything and you are going to the police on Monday if he doesn't turn himself in."

"Do I tell him who I am? I mean if he asks?" Mia asked, peering at Ryan.

"No. Don't tell him who you are other than a friend of Holly's. I'm sure he'll check the number and find all he needs to get here from the college registry." Ryan put a hand on hers. "You won't be in any danger. James has already called in officers to start watching our place tonight. You just can't go outside alone until he is caught."

Mia nodded. She dialed the number, pushed speaker, and set the phone on the table as if it had suddenly become red hot.

"If this is a scammer go try someone who is gullible."

"I'm not a scammer. I'm a friend of Holly Garvie's. She told me everything. How you met in the library, she was pregnant, and you were going to leave your wife." Mia swallowed and said, "Only that was a lie, wasn't it? I know you killed Holly. I'm going to the police on Monday, now that I've figured it out."

"Lady, you're crazy. If you call me again, I'll see that the cops come find you."

"Good! That will make it easier for me to tell them what you did to Holly," Mia said with the wrath of someone who had something stolen.

"Listen to me you—"

Someone on the other end of the conversation said something. "I'll be right there," the man said in a calm voice. The quiet dragged for two seconds and he hissed into the phone. "What's your name?"

"I'm not having you come after me. I'm just telling you to turn yourself in. I don't want to be mixed up in this any more than I already am." She hit the end button and smiled.

Shandra hugged her. "Well done."

Ryan grinned and motioned to her. "I told you she could do a good job."

James shook his head. "That last line

will definitely catch his attention on who made the call."

"Haven't I lost enough family without you putting my sister in the sights of a killer!"

Shandra tried to stop Jayden as he stormed out of the room and out the back door. When she took a step to go after him, Mia whipped around her.

"Let me talk to him. He's still reeling from what happened with our family." She disappeared into the mudroom and then the outside door thumped.

"I see why you said to have Mia make the call. Jayden does have trouble controlling his emotions," James said.

"He saw his parents right after they were killed. Both of them. He had nightmares after seeing Holly's body." Ryan ran a hand over the back of his neck. Shandra knew he was regretting using Mia as bait. Not because he feared for her but what it was doing to Jayden.

"He'll be fine. Mia knows how to talk

him into her way of thinking," Shandra said. Hoping this didn't end up being the one time Mia couldn't make him see this was the only way to get him completely removed from the police suspect list.

Ryan had a long talk with Shandra, then Mia, and finally Jayden about how Mia wasn't going to be in harm's way. There would be a deputy on the last road off the county road before their house to watch for Cotter's vehicle and inform the others when it was seen. Three other law enforcement officers would be scattered about the property. One in the barn to watch the back side of the house, one in the pottery shed to watch from the south, and one on the north side of the house.

Now he sat in the great room talking to Claude and waiting for the rest of their Christmas Eve guests to arrive.

"I'm thinking about selling the feed store. Everyone else is running it these days. Lil and I are thinking about going somewhere warm from January to March. Neither one of us likes this cold weather anymore," Claude said.

"There's nothing wrong with that," Ryan said, noticing Mia frowning at her cell phone. "Excuse me a minute." He stood and walked over to the rocking chair where Mia sat with her cat on her lap. "What's up?"

She handed him her phone. The text message said, *Stay away from the cops or your brother will go down for it.*

"I can't tell Jayden about this. He's already mad that I'm messing with a crazy person." Mia peered up into his eyes. Fear glinted in her brown irises.

"You are both safe. Remember, it's the police who are trying to catch him. They know Jayden didn't do it." Ryan handed the phone back. "But let's keep this from Jayden."

She nodded. "I'll go help Mom and Lil in the kitchen."

The door knocker banged.

Ryan answered the door and welcomed

in Ruthie, Maxwell, and Donny and saw headlights coming up the lane. That would be the Porters. "Come on in. Lil and Claude are here already."

He helped them out of the coats. While Maxwell and Claude talked and Donnie and Ruthie went into the kitchen, Ryan put the coats in the closet and texted James to let him know Cotter was upset.

He walked out of the closet and walked over to the front window to see what was keeping the Porter family. There weren't any lights or any sign of their vehicle. He hadn't been crazy. There had been a vehicle coming up the lane behind the Treats.

"Maxwell, was that Miranda and Alex following you in?" Ryan asked, scanning the house for Mia.

"I thought it was them but they should have come to the door by now." Maxwell rose to his nearly seven-foot height and strode to the other large plate glass window. "I don't see anything out there."

"Mia, Jayden!" Ryan called out.

Jayden stepped from the kitchen with his hands covered in flour.

"Is your sister in there?" Ryan asked.

"No, she and Lil went out to look at the horses." Jayden started for the hallway but Ryan moved by him and blocked the door to the mudroom.

"Damn!" He pulled out his phone and called James. "Mia's outside with Lil. A car came up the driveway and now I don't see it. I'm going out to look for them. Tell the men staked out to also keep an eye open." He ended the call and opened the door to the mudroom.

"I'm going with you," Jayden said, grabbing his coat.

"Stay in here. We don't know what Cotter might do."

Maxwell pushed Jayden into the room and asked, "What's going on?"

"Ask Shandra, but I want you and Jayden to stay in the house and protect Shandra and our guests." Ryan gave Jayden's arm a squeeze and opened the door.

Boom! A shotgun blast shredded the stillness of the night.

Ryan ran toward the barn. He flung open the barn door and spotted someone kneeling on the ground.

"Get up you no-good murderer. I didn't hit nothin' but your leg," Lil said loudly as she came around the back of the Jeep.

Two bright lights came through the door behind Ryan seconds after a light bobbed down the ladder to the loft.

"That woman is crazy. I'm pressing charges!" Shouted the man holding his leg sitting on the floor of the barn.

"Lil, take Mia into the house," Ryan said above the man's yelling.

"She's already there," Lil said, pointing her shotgun at the man on the ground. "I told her as soon as I shot the man to take off for the house."

"I didn't pass her?" Ryan said, worried that Cotter had brought Skylar with him.

"She went out through the corral and behind the pottery shed." Lil finally cradled the shotgun in her arms as the state policemen handcuffed and brought the man to his feet.

As they were walking toward the house a vehicle slid to a stop behind Maxwell's SUV. The door flung open and James rushed out into the snow and darkness toward them.

"He's detained," Ryan said.

"Take him to the Huckleberry Station. We'll question him there," James said, motioning for the staters to put the man in the back of the deputy's car that followed James up the road.

"What happened?" James asked.

Ryan led him into the house where Lil had already disappeared. "I honestly don't know. We'll find out together."

Chapter Seventeen

Shandra hugged Mia tight when she burst into the house and said Lil shot Cotter. Now they were all gathered in the great room, after having helped the Porters into the house and settled the children watching a movie in Jayden's room.

"Why did you go outside, Mia?" James asked.

Shandra gave her hand a squeeze. "Always tell the truth."

Mia drew in a deep breath and said, "I got a text from Cotter. It sounded like he was coming tonight. I just had this feeling. I'd told Lil what was going on when she caught me staring at the text in the laundry room. She said when all the guests arrived, we'd go out and look at the horses and come up with a plan." Mia shrugged. "Two cars came in together so we figured it was the guests. Lil suggested we go look at the horses so we did. We'd barely got to the barn and Lil said someone was in there because the horses sounded agitated. She told me to put my phone on record and if she shot the gun to get myself into the house immediately."

Lil nodded and said, "I crept into my old bunk room and pulled my shotgun off the wall. I left it here for Shandra to keep away varmints. When I came back out, I saw a man holding onto Mia's arm and asking her what she knew. I waited until he made a comment that sounded like he did kill that girl and I made a noise, he let go of Mia and I shot him in the leg so he couldn't go after her or getaway." She put a hand on Claude's shoulder. "That was the most fun I've had in a long time." Her husband grinned at her.

"Can I see your phone?" James asked.

Mia handed it over.

James stood and motioned to Ryan. "Is there a place we can go and listen to this where no one else can hear? It is evidence in this case."

Ryan led him down the hall to the mudroom.

Shandra pulled Mia to her feet and motioned for Jayden to join them. They had a group hug and Shandra said, "Let's go dish up dinner."

The house became a flurry of motion and talking as everyone filed through the kitchen gathering food and children before sitting around the table in the dining area.

Shandra put an arm around Lil when they were the last two in the kitchen. "Thank you for taking care of Mia."

"You know those two are my only grandchildren. I'd never let harm come to them. Not as long as I can lift a shotgun." Lil hugged Shandra back and she felt the older woman shake just a little. The whole thing had scared her more than she was letting on.

"Hey, you two, shouldn't you be with our guests," Ryan asked, picking up a plate and filling it with food.

Lil picked up her plate and left the kitchen.

"Well, did Mia get enough for them to charge Cotter?" Shandra asked.

"Not enough to charge him but enough that James can interview him until he does get all the information." Ryan kissed Shandra's cheek. "I'm glad I married a strong woman who has raised a strong daughter."

Shandra smiled. "You didn't have a choice given all your sisters and your mom."

"I'm glad of that as well."

~*~

Grandmother walked along a large pond poking a long stick into the water.

Shandra stood up on the top of the bank. The smell of asphalt and oil made her nose wrinkle. "What are you doing?" she asked her ella. "Why are you poking at the water?"

"Things are hidden in watery depths." Grandmother swirled her stick and pulled it out. A piece of clothing dangled from the end. "Is Skylar's body hidden in a pond?" Shandra asked.

Grandmother waved her stick around like a wizard. "Look. See." Grandmother disappeared. Shandra studied the area and realized she was at a place that made asphalt. There was large excavation equipment and a smell that she recognized from construction crews fixing roads. As she peered intently at the area the ground around her shook.

"Mom, wake up!" Mia's voice drifted into Shandra's dream. "Come on! Santa brought you something." Mia pulled on Shandra's arm.

"Just a minute. Let me wake up. I'll be out in five minutes," Shandra opened her eyes and couldn't miss the excitement shining in her daughter's eyes. "What's this about Santa bringing me something?" she asked, slipping her feet into her slippers and pulling a robe on over her pajamas.

"You'll see. Come on. Ryan has the cinnamon rolls in the oven. We thought we'd let you sleep in since you were up late cleaning up from the company and getting ready for all the Greers today."

Shandra listened to Mia as she washed her face and brushed her hair back into a ponytail. She really wanted to find a notebook and write down what she'd seen in the dream. But the twins didn't know about her dreams and she wasn't going to tell anyone but Ryan about this latest one.

"OK, let's go. But I don't know why a person of your age would be so excited about Santa coming. You know he isn't real."

Mia opened the door and stepped aside.

Shandra's first thought was 'How long did I sleep?' It appeared the house was full of Ryan's family. From his parents down to his nieces and nephews. She scanned all the faces hunting for her husband. The group parted and he stepped forward carrying the fluffiest, cutest red puppy she'd ever laid eyes on.

"Merry Christmas, Shandra," Ryan said, placing the puppy in her arms.

The ball of fur licked her cheek and she fell in love. A tear slid down her face. "How did you know I was needing this?"

Ryan motioned to his father. "Dad called me and said he found the perfect gift for me to give you. We all know how much you loved Sheba. And how lonesome you are when you come out here to work on your pottery. Now you'll have company when I can't be here." Ryan kissed her.

She returned the kiss and smiled at everyone. "You're early for Christmas dinner."

They all laughed.

Colleen stepped forward. "We wanted to be present when you received the puppy. And to help with the meal. We have all missed Jayden and Mia and wanted to spend more time with them."

The smaller cousins ran over and hugged the twins. The two smiled and hugged them back.

"I'll get dressed and come make you breakfast," Shandra said, still hugging the wiggly puppy.

"We have it under control," Cathleen said. "You can dress, and we'll exchange gifts while the breakfast casserole is cooking."

"Thank you. I'll only be a few minutes." She grasped Ryan's hand. "I have something to tell you," she whispered, leading him into the bedroom.

"That you love me?" he offered, closing the door behind him.

Shandra laughed. "That, and Grandmother came to me in a dream. I think Skylar's body is in a pond near an asphalt plant. Maybe you can let James know that and see if that scares something out of Cotter."

"Hmmm, not sure how to make him

listen when I can't tell him you had a dream. But I'll think of something." He took the puppy from her. "Do you like her? She's a Chow poodle."

"She's adorable. Thank you and your dad. But you go make that call to James and I'll get dressed." She pulled the puppy out of his arms. "And leave Noel with me."

Ryan smiled and left the bedroom.

Shandra talked and played with Noel as she dressed. The only thing that could make today better would be learning they had arrested Dean Cotter.

Epilogue

Shandra stood on the front porch with Noel in her arms and holding back tears.

"They'll be home during the four-day weekend in January," Ryan said, as he waved at the twins heading back for college.

"I know but I miss them already. They have been a blessing to our marriage and lives." Shandra wiped the tear that tickled her cheek onto Noel's red fur.

"That they have." Ryan put an arm around her shoulders. "I can hang out here with you and Noel for a few more days. Since the Holly Garvie homicide is wrapped up, I'm free."

She nudged him. "You were free even when it was an ongoing investigation since you were pulled from it."

He studied her. "You know I couldn't let it be with our kids in the middle of it."

She kissed his cheek. "Yes, I wouldn't have wanted you to back off, either. But I'm glad James was able to get that security guard to finally confess."

"It was James telling him they knew Skylar was in the pond. Then he sent some officers over to dredge a pond at an asphalt plant not far from the college. They came up with Skylar's body." Ryan turned them around and they walked into the house.

Shandra placed Noel on the floor and faced Ryan, "Did James ask how you knew that's where the body was?"

"Yeah, I told him Mia had figured it out by something Cotter had said to her. Thankfully, he didn't ask any more questions." Ryan sat on the couch and motioned for Shandra to join him. "I know you like the visits from your grandmother, but I hope she stays out of your dreams from now on. We don't need any more of our family caught up in a homicide investigation."

Shandra sat beside him and rested her head on his shoulder. "I agree. I do enjoy her visits but they always get us caught up in murder."

Noel bounced on her back legs, trying to get on Shandra's lap. She helped the puppy up and said, "One of these days, you are going to be too big for this."

Ryan laughed. "And you will keep allowing her to sit on the couch with her front paws on your lap."

"Yes, I will. Because there is nothing better than being near those you love."

I hope you enjoyed *Christmas Chaos*. If so, please leave a review or tell someone about the book. While I was ready to leave Huckleberry when I wrote the last book in the series, *Vanishing Dream*, it was fun to return to write this Christmas novella.

If you liked this and haven't already read a book in the Shandra Higheagle Mystery series, please try book one, *Double Duplicity*. And if you have read the series, check out my other mystery series, Gabriel Hawke Novels and Spotted Pony Casino Mysteries. You can find them all at my website, hhttps://www.patyjager.net or at your favorite place to purchase books. Just ask for them. All bookstores can purchase my books through their usual outlet. Or ask for them at your local library. They are all available in ebook, print, and audio.

Thank you for purchasing this book!

Thank you for purchasing this Windtree Press
publication. For other books of the heart, please
visit our website at www.windtreepress.com.

For questions or more information contact us
at info@windtreepress.com.

Windtree Press
www.windtreepress.com

Corvallis, OR